Cara

THE WORLD OF NORM
NORM
MAY BE CONTAGIOUS

ORCHARD BOOKS
338 Euston Road, London NW1 3BH
Orchard Books Australia
Level 17/207 Kent Street, Sydney, NSW 2000

First published in 2013 by Orchard Books

A Paperback Original

ISBN 978 1 40832 839 2

A CIP catalogue record for this book is available from the British Library.

5 7 9 10 8 6 4

Printed in Great Britain by CPI Group

Orchard Books is a division of Hachette Children's Books,
an Hachette UK company.

www.hachette.co.uk

JONATHAN MERES

THE WORLD OF NORM

MAY BE CONTAGIOUS

ORCHARD

To my big brother –
who isn't the least bit annoying.

CHAPTER 1

Norm knew it was going to be one of those days when he woke up and found a bit of sweet corn in his left ear. He wouldn't have minded, but he didn't actually **like** sweet corn. What was going on? wondered Norm. And why was everything **so** quiet? Had the rest of the family moved house again without telling him? Be flipping typical if they had.

Rather than investigating though – and finding out whether the rest of the family really **had** moved house without telling him – Norm simply brushed the sweet corn onto his bedroom carpet and lay back down to read a mountain biking magazine instead. It **was** Saturday after all. There was no particular hurry to get up. Not that there ever **was** a particular hurry to get up as far as Norm was concerned. But on Saturday, there was even **less** of a hurry to get up than usual. Besides, the only thing Norm had planned that day was to go biking with his best friend, Mikey. But that wasn't till after lunch. And lunch wasn't going to happen till after breakfast. And breakfast wasn't going to happen till after Norm had got up. Not unless someone brought him breakfast in bed it wasn't, anyway.

Norm put down his mountain biking magazine and listened for a moment. The house really was **very** quiet indeed. It certainly **sounded** like he was all alone, in which case, breakfast in bed was looking increasingly unlikely.

Norm sighed. Some people were just **so** flipping inconsiderate.

So where exactly *were* his mum and dad and his two little brothers? wondered Norm. And when would they be back? Assuming that they **would** be back at some point, of course and they hadn't been abducted by aliens, or something. It wasn't that Norm was **scared** being home alone. He actually quite **liked** being home alone. But sooner or later, the novelty always wore off. Usually round about the time Norm needed food.

Or clean pants.
Or possibly both.

The **best** thing about being home alone as far as Norm was concerned was that he could pretend he

was an only child again, like he had been, back in the day. When life had been sweet and the world had revolved around him, and him alone.

But then his mum had gone and ruined everything by having Brian – AKA **the** most annoying brother on the entire flipping planet. Then to make matters even **worse**, a couple of years after **that**, she went and had Dave – aka the **second** most annoying brother on the entire flipping planet. Life, for Norm, had never been the same since. The only consolation was that his parents were now far too ancient to have any **more** children. Or at least Norm flipping **hoped** they were anyway. The

thought of his mum and dad **kissing** was gross enough – let alone the thought of them doing anything else.

The phone rang downstairs. Norm sighed again. Who could that be, calling at this time of the morning? Not that Norm had the faintest idea what time it actually was. And not that it actually mattered who it was anyway. There was more chance of Norm learning ballet than there was of him actually getting out of bed to answer the phone. Why should **he** answer the phone? It wouldn't be for him.

Gordon flipping Bennet! thought Norm, as the phone continued to ring and ring and ring. Wasn't it **obvious** by now that no one was In?

"SHUT UP!" yelled Norm, getting angrier and angrier.

That worked. The phone suddenly stopped ringing. Norm resumed reading.

"Hello?" called a voice a few moments later.

Uh? thought Norm. Who was that? Certainly not his mum or dad, and not one of his brothers either!

"Anyone home?" said the voice, a bit louder.

It couldn't be, thought Norm. Surely not? She wouldn't flipping dare! **Would** she?

"Hello, **Norman!**" said Chelsea, standing framed in the doorway. "What time do you call this, then?"

"Time you got out of my flipping bedroom!" shouted Norm.

"No need to be so ungrateful," said Chelsea.

Norm couldn't believe it. She'd waltzed uninvited into **his** house and now she expected him to be **grateful**?

"I'll call the police!"

Chelsea grinned. "What will you call them?"

"Uh?" said Norm.

"Nice PJs by the way," said Chelsea.

"What?" said Norm.

"Your pyjamas?"

Norm looked down. He just **had** to be wearing the ones with the flipping dinosaur pattern, didn't he? Not a good look when you were nearly thirteen.

"I'm only wearing these cos my other ones are in the wash."

"It's OK, **Norman**," said Chelsea. "Dinosaurs are cool."

"Really?" said Norm doubtfully. "You think so?"

"Absolutely," said Chelsea. "When you're five!"

She burst out laughing.

"Just get out," said Norm.

"Don't you want to know what I'm doing here?" said Chelsea.

Actually, thought Norm, now she came to mention it he **would** quite like to know what Chelsea was doing in his bedroom.

"Go on then."

"The front door was open."

"What?" said Norm.

"The front door," said Chelsea. "It was wide open."

"Yeah, but that doesn't mean you can just walk in!"

Chelsea shrugged. "I saw everybody rushing out and getting in the car."

"Everybody?" said Norm.

Chelsea nodded. "Even the dog!"

"When?"

"Just now," said Chelsea. "I'm surprised you didn't hear."

Norm was surprised he hadn't heard too until suddenly he remembered the bit of sweet corn in his ear.

"I was just making sure everything was OK in case something bad had happened, that's all," said Chelsea. "Just being a good neighbour, **Norman**!"

Just being flipping nosy more like, thought Norm. If Chelsea **really** wanted to be a good neighbour she'd flipping move. She was **SO** annoying.

"Shhh!" said Norm suddenly.

Chelsea looked puzzled. "But I didn't say anything."

"Shhhhhhh!!!" said Norm again, more urgently. "Listen!"

They listened. Somewhere nearby – faint and muffled – a mobile was ringing.

"Aren't you going to get it?" said Chelsea.

"Dunno where it is," said Norm.

Chelsea walked further into Norm's room and looked around. "I'm not surprised. Look at the state of this place."

Norm was gobsmacked. "What?"

"Seriously, **Norman**. I've seen tidier rubbish dumps."

Norm couldn't decide what he found more infuriating. The way Chelsea continually overemphasised his name like it was the funniest thing she'd ever heard, or the fact that she'd actually had the nerve to criticise the state of his room. Either way, he knew he couldn't let it wind him up. He needed to find his phone, and quickly. What if it was Mikey?

Norm leapt out of bed and headed towards the source of the sound. Or, at least, as far as he could tell he did, anyway. He hated to admit it, but Chelsea did have a point. His room *could* do with a bit of a tidy. Well – a *lot* of a tidy actually.

After several unsuccessful attempts, Norm eventually located his phone underneath a pile of clothes on the floor and answered it.

"Hello?"

Norm looked at Chelsea. Was she just going to stand there and stare all day, or what?

"Oh. Hi, Mum."

Chelsea giggled.

"Shut up!"

Norm listened for a moment. "No, not you, Mum! I was talking to Chelsea."

"Hi!" squealed Chelsea.

"What, Mum?" said Norm. "No, you see, the front door was open. She thought something might have happened."

Chelsea grinned.

Norm sighed. "Do I have to, Mum?"

"What?" said Chelsea.

"Mum says to tell you you're a good neighbour," muttered Norm, through gritted teeth.

"See?" said Chelsea.

"Where are you?" said Norm.

There was a pause.

"The vet?" said Norm. "Why? What's wrong with Brian?"

There was another pause.

"What?" said Norm. "No, it was just a joke, Mum!"

Norm listened.

"'Kay, Mum. See you soon, Mum. Bye, Mum."

Norm ended the call. Chelsea looked at him expectantly.

"Well?"

"The dog's ill," said Norm.

"Well, duh," said Chelsea.

"What?" said Norm.

"I meant, what's the **matter** with the dog?"

"Oh, right," said Norm. "He's got a little…"

"A little what?" grinned Chelsea.

"Bug," said Norm.

"Ah, that's a shame," said Chelsea. "Poor thing."

Norm pulled a face. "Poor thing?"

"He's so sweet," said Chelsea in a squeaky baby voice.

"Sweet?" said Norm. "He's disgusting!"

"Ah, he's **not**," said Chelsea.

"Flipping *is*. All he does is eat and sleep and lick his own…"

Norm suddenly stopped. What was he doing even **having** this conversation?

"What?" said Chelsea.

Norm shrugged. "What do you mean, **what?**"

"What do you **mean**, what do I mean, **what?**"

"Can you just go, please?" said Norm.

"Pardon?" said Chelsea.

"Get out!" said Norm, a bit louder.

"What do you say?" grinned Chelsea.

"NOW!" yelled Norm.

"All right, **Norman**! Keep your hair on!" said Chelsea, disappearing out of the room and heading for the stairs.

At last, thought Norm. Peace and flipping quiet.

"It's OK! I'll let myself out!" yelled Chelsea.

But Norm wasn't listening. He'd had a sudden thought. If he asked nicely, then perhaps Chelsea might...

The front door suddenly slammed. It was too late. It looked like Norm was actually going to have to get his **own** breakfast.

Flipping typical.

CHAPTER 2

The first Norm knew of the dog puke on the bathroom floor was when he slipped on it. Up until that moment, he'd been making steady, if unspectacular, progress towards the toilet – a journey he'd made literally several hundred times since they'd moved a few months previously. Norm hadn't been happy at the time. He wasn't much happier *now* if the truth were told, but he'd grudgingly accepted that they were probably here to stay and that there wasn't much he could do about it anyway. This was *real* life, not some flipping book – with its ridiculous cast of characters and equally ridiculous storylines. But that wasn't the point. The point was, Norm was pretty familiar with the route to and from the toilet. He certainly hadn't had any incidents or accidents before – apart from nearly peeing in his dad's wardrobe. He wasn't *expecting* to have any incidents or accidents in the future. But then he hadn't **expected** the encounter with Chelsea either. So you just never knew.

When it happened, it happened very quickly. Much **too** quickly for Norm to register **what** was actually happening at the time. It was only afterwards – when he was sitting on the floor holding his wrist – that Norm realised he must have trodden in something that wasn't usually there. Something that **shouldn't** have been there in the first place.

"Ow," said Norm, to no one in particular. Not that there was anyone around to say it to anyway. Norm was still home alone as far as he could tell.

It was the smell that hit Norm first. A smell quite unlike any other smell that Norm had ever smelled before – or **wanted** to smell ever again, for that matter. Norm was no stranger to bad smells. He had two younger brothers, after all. **And** Mikey had hormones. But this was somehow different. This wasn't just **unpleasant** – it was positively evil. Like something had died and remained undetected for several months.

It was the damp feeling on his bum that hit Norm second – as whatever he'd slipped on and subsequently **landed** on eventually soaked through his pyjama bottoms.

"Aw, no," groaned Norm, who by now had a pretty good idea of exactly what it was he'd slipped on. "Flipping dog!"

A car door slammed outside as Norm began struggling to get to his feet. He was still struggling to get to his feet when he heard the front door slam, followed by the sound of footsteps on the stairs.

"I need the toilet," said Brian, appearing in the bathroom doorway a few seconds later.

"Well, tough," said Norm.

"What?" said Brian.

"You heard," said Norm.

Brian observed Norm for a moment. "What are you doing?"

Norm sighed. "What does it *look* like I'm doing?"

Brian shrugged. "Standing up?"

"So why flipping *ask*, Brian, you flipping freak?"

"But..."

"But **what**?" snapped Norm.

"What were you doing sitting down?" said Brian. "In the bathroom?"

"Gordon flipping Bennet," muttered Norm. "I wasn't sitting down."

"Uh?" said Brian. "What **were** you doing then?"

"I wasn't doing **anything**, you doughnut!" said Norm. "I slipped, OK?"

"Why?"

Norm looked at his middle brother. Of all the stupid questions he'd ever asked, this was definitely one of the stupidest. "Why?"

Brian nodded.

"**Why** did I slip?"

Brian nodded again.

"You should flipping know," said Norm.

"Should I?" said Brian, looking puzzled. "Why's that then?"

"It's **your** flipping dog!" yelled Norm.

Brian pulled a face. "What's John got to do with it?"

Norm took a deep breath. "He threw up on the floor. **That's** what I slipped on."

"Oh right," said Brian. "He must have been trying to get to the toilet."

"What?" said Norm.

"He must have been trying to get to the toilet, but didn't quite make it."

Norm **almost** smiled. "You're not actually **serious**, are you?"

"John's more intelligent than you think, Norman!" said Brian indignantly.

"Oh yeah?" said Norm. "Well if he's *that* intelligent, how come he doesn't just *sit* on the toilet when he needs a flipping dump, then?"

"Don't be ridiculous."

What? thought Norm. *He* was being ridiculous? What flipping planet was Brian living on if he honestly believed John was trying to get to the toilet before he was sick? More likely he was trying to get to the toilet because he was thirsty. Dogs were *so* flipping disgusting.

"Anyway, it's not my fault," said Brian.

"Well it's not *my* flipping fault!" said Norm.

"What isn't?" said Norm's mum, appearing in the doorway.

"That I slipped," said Norm.

Norm's mum looked puzzled. "It's not your fault that you slipped?"

Norm sighed. Wasn't it screamingly obvious that he was in severe pain here? Well, a **bit** of pain anyway. OK – slight discomfort. But even so...

"I slipped on some sick."

"John's sick," explained Brian.

"Oh, I see," said Norm's mum. "Are you OK, love?"

"No, I'm not OK, actually," said Norm. "I've hurt my wrist."

"Let me see."

Norm held up his wrist for his mum to look at.

"Ooh, yes."

"What?" said Norm.

"Well, it *is* a bit swollen," said Norm's mum. "No biking for you today, love!"

"What?" said Norm.

"You're supposed to be going biking with Mikey, aren't you?"

"Yeah, but..."

"No buts I'm afraid, love," said Norm's mum.

"But..."

"Uh-uh," said Norm's mum, wagging an index finger. "Completely out of the question. You'd have to ride one-handed!"

"That's easy, Mum!" protested Norm. "I do it all the time!"

"I don't care if it's easy or not, Norman," said Norm's mum. "I'm not letting you ride your bike today and that's all there is to it. You've already hurt your wrist. We don't want you doing even **more** damage now, do we?

Norm glared thunderously at Brian. Talking of serious damage...

"What?" said Brian innocently. "It's not **my** fault!"

Norm could feel himself beginning to bubble up and boil inside. Biking, to Norm, was like eating and breathing and going to the toilet. It was something he **needed** to do. But he could tell there was no point arguing. His mum had clearly made up her mind. There'd be no biking for Norm today and that was flipping that.

"Do you know you've got sick on your pyjamas?" said Brian.

"Yes, I **do** know, thanks," said Norm irritably.

"It looks like you've just…"

"I **know** what it looks like, Brian, OK?"

"OK," said Brian. "I was just…"

"Shhh!" said Norm. "Listen."

They listened. A phone was ringing. **Norm's** phone was ringing.

"I'd better get that," said Norm.

"No, I'll get it," said Norm's mum, disappearing off down the landing. "You get out of those dirty pyjamas and get yourself cleaned up, love."

Norm turned slowly and deliberately to face Brian. "Still need the toilet?"

"Wait for me, Mum!" called Brian, heading out of the door.

CHAPTER 3

Norm twisted around to try and look at his sick-covered bum. What **had** John been eating? Whatever it was, it looked pretty flipping disgusting. Well, it did now anyway. Then again, thought Norm, **anything** that a dog had eaten and then thrown up again was always going to look pretty flipping disgusting.

Hang on, thought Norm, looking more closely at his bum. Was that what he **thought** it was? **Sweet corn**? What was going on?

"Norman?" called Norm's mum.

"Yeah?"

"Get in your room now!"

Gordon flipping Bennet, thought Norm, setting off. Either she wanted him to get cleaned up or she wanted to see him in his room! He couldn't do both. Not at the same time anyway.

"I said *now*, Norman!"

"What is it?" said Norm.

Norm's mum spun round to find Norm standing in the doorway. "What *is* it?"

Norm nodded.

"What do you *think* it is?"

Norm shrugged. "Dunno, Mum."

"Would you like a clue?" said Norm's mum.

Great, thought Norm. Nothing he liked better first thing in the flipping morning than a game of

twenty flipping questions.
What next? Musical chairs?
Pass the flipping parcel?

"We couldn't find your
phone," said Brian.

"Yeah? So?" said Norm.

"So it's about time you
tidied your room!" said
Norm's mum.

"'Kay, Mum. I'll do it later."

"You will *not* do it later, Norman!"

Norm was confused. "When will I do it, then?"

"Now!"

Norm sighed. Just when he thought the day couldn't possibly get any worse – it just flipping had.

"But..."

"But what, love?"

Norm thought for a moment. He needed an excuse and he needed one fast.

"I've hurt my wrist."

Norm's mum smiled.

"I **have**!" squeaked Norm.

"I *know* you have, love," said Norm's mum. "It's not broken though, is it?"

"What?" said Norm.

"It's hardly life-threatening."

"It **might** be!" said Norm.

"You seemed to think you could still go biking a minute ago," said Norm's mum.

"That's different," said Norm.

"No, it's not," said Brian.

"What?" said Norm. "You think biking and tidying your room is the same thing? What *are* you, Brian? **Stupid** or something?"

"No," said Brian. "But you said you could ride your bike one-handed."

"Yeah? So?" said Norm.

Brian shrugged. "So you could tidy your room one-handed."

Norm took a deep breath and let it out again slowly. Brian was right and he knew it. More significantly, Brian was right and his **mum** knew it. If Norm was fit enough to go **biking**, he was fit enough to tidy his room. That wasn't the point though. The point was Norm actually **wanted** to go biking, whereas he had no desire whatsoever to tidy his flipping room. It was **SO** annoying!

"Well?" said Norm's mum.

"What?" said Norm.

"You'd better get cracking, hadn't you?"

Norm sighed with resignation. He was fighting a losing battle. His mum was right. He better **had** get cracking.

"Can I get some money, Mum?"

"Pardon?" said Norm's mum.

"Can I get some money?"

Norm's mum pulled a face. "What for?"

"Dunno yet," said Norm. "Sweets?"

"That's *not* what I meant," said Norm's mum. "I meant **why** should I give you some money?"

Why? thought Norm. Gordon flipping Bennet. Wasn't it screamingly obvious? Did he have to spell **everything** out?

"For tidying my room."

For a moment or two, Norm's mum seemed genuinely lost for words.

"You **are** joking aren't you, love?"

Joking? thought Norm. He'd never been so serious in all his life. Having to tidy his room was bad enough. But being expected to do it for **free**? What was this? Flipping Victorian times or something?

"You actually want **paying** for tidying your own room?"

"Er, yeah," said Norm. "If you don't mind, Mum."

"I don't mind at all, love," said Norm's mum breezily.

Norm hadn't expected his mum to cave in **quite** so quickly. "Really?"

"Sure. Why not?" said Norm's mum, heading for the doorway. "You'll get paid as soon as *I* start getting paid for all the cooking, cleaning and laundry I do. Now if you'll excuse me."

"What?" said Norm.

"I've got work to do," said Norm's mum.

Norm stood to one side to let his mum get past.

"And Norman?"

"Yeah?"

"So have you."

Norm watched his mum disappear down the stairs. He might have flipping known she was being sarcastic. It was *SO* flipping unfair.

"Ha, ha!" sang Brian.

"Shut your face, Brian, you little freak!" hissed Norm.

CHAPTER 4

Once Norm had got dressed – and put his puke-stained PJs in the laundry basket – he lay back down on his bed to consider his options. Clearly his **first** option was to do a runner. If Norm somehow managed to sneak out of the house and leg it before anyone noticed, he wouldn't actually *have* to tidy his room. At least, not straight away he wouldn't anyway. He'd still have to do it at **some** point. Just not any point soon.

Unless, of course – and this was Norm's **second** option – he got someone else to do it *for* him. Like one of his brothers for instance. Preferably Brian. Brian owed him one. Actually, thought Norm, Brian owed him more than one. So did Dave, for that matter. After all, Dave could be pretty annoying at times too. But Brian was off the flipping scale annoying. Thanks to **Brian**, Norm hadn't been able to wangle his way out of tidying his room. He was going to have to pay for that **somehow**.

The third – and, by some considerable distance, Norm's *least* favourite – option was to actually do it. Just tidy up his room and get it over with. Because unless his mum suddenly ordered some kind of fully automatic room-tidying robot off one of the shopping channels, **someone** was going to have to do it sooner or later.

Norm sighed. He wasn't a happy bunny. Even by unhappy bunny standards he wasn't a happy bunny. But deep down inside, Norm knew it was not only the **sensible** option, but also the **right** option. It was **so** unfair though, thought Norm. Why should *he* have to tidy his **own** flipping room? Frankly it was outrageous – not to mention a breach of basic human rights.

Had he not been punished enough by not being allowed to go biking?

Norm propped himself up on one elbow and looked around. It wasn't **that** messy, was it? Just a couple of things scattered on the floor. You could still make out bits of carpet here and there, couldn't you? So what was all the fuss about? And anyway, thought Norm, it wasn't **his** fault there was nowhere to put stuff! If he had some flipping furniture he could actually put things away!

From the garden came the sound of excited yelps. Norm **assumed** it was John, although, come to think of it, Dave could get pretty hyper depending on how many Haribos he'd eaten. He'd scoffed a whole packet of fried eggs once when he was tiny and gone **completely** bonkers – buzzing around and bashing into stuff like a demented bluebottle.

Norm got out of bed, walked to the window and pulled open the curtains.

BUZZZ

Sure enough, it **was** John, rushing around in ever decreasing circles in an increasingly vain attempt to catch up with his tail.

Flipping dog, thought Norm. Didn't look very ill now, did it? Not after spewing up all over the bathroom floor. It was **SO** flipping annoying. What was even *more* annoying was the fact that it was such a beautiful day. Why couldn't it have been peeing down with rain and blowing a flipping gale? It wouldn't have **mattered** that he couldn't go biking then, would it? He'd have probably been stuck inside anyway. It was going to be even **more** frustrating now!

Norm flexed his sore wrist. It was already beginning to feel better. He'd be fine biking. If he did a really good job of tidying his room, maybe he could still persuade his mum to let him go. But before Norm could start, his phone rang again. But where from? wondered Norm. Where had he chucked it after he'd spoken to his mum earlier on? It **sounded** like it was coming from under his bed.

Norm got down on his hands and knees and looked. His phone **was** under his bed. But so was something else. Something Norm was only too familiar with. The unmistakeable shape of a cardboard pizza box!

Uh? thought Norm. What was **that** doing there? How long had it **been** there? He couldn't remember eating pizza in bed. Not recently anyway.

Crawling under the bed to investigate more

closely, Norm noticed two things. Firstly, that there was still some pizza left in the box – and secondly, that his phone had stopped ringing.

Norm looked at the screen to see who the missed call was from. Not that he actually **needed** to look. Norm knew it would be Mikey. And sure enough it **was**. Probably just to confirm arrangements for meeting up later. He'd be disappointed when he found out that Norm couldn't make it. But that wasn't **Norm's** flipping fault, thought Norm, hitting speed dial.

"All right?" said Norm when Mikey answered his phone a second later.

Norm listened.

"Er, yeah, about that, Mikey. I can't."

Norm listened some more.

"What? No, well, I've hurt my wrist, haven't I?"

Norm pulled a face.

"It's not **my** flipping fault! I slipped on some dog puke!"

There was an explosion of laughter from down the line.

"Shut up, Mikey! It's not flipping funny!"

HA HA HA!

END

"Norman?" said Norm's dad from the doorway, making Norm jump and bump his head on the underside of the bed.

"Ouch!" said Norm.

"Are you OK?"

Norm sighed. No, he flipping **wasn't** OK! What kind of stupid question was **that**?

"What are you doing under there?"

"Talking to Mikey."

"What?" said Norm's dad.

Gordon flipping Bennet, thought Norm. "On the **phone**, Dad!"

"Oh right, I see! I thought you meant..."

"Catch you later, Mikey," said Norm, ringing off.

"Mum needs a cauliflower," said Norm's dad as Norm crawled out from underneath his bed and stood up, rubbing his head.

"What?" said Norm.

"Mum needs a cauliflower."

Norm pulled a face. So what if his mum **did** need a cauliflower? What had that got to do with **him**?

"**I** haven't got one."

"Don't get smart with **me**, Norman."

Norm was genuinely confused. He **hadn't** got a cauliflower. He **hated** cauliflower. And anyway, if his mum wanted one **that** badly, why didn't she just order one off the flipping telly?

"Go and see if Grandpa's got one."

"What?" said Norm.

"At the allotments."

"Oh right," said Norm. "You should've said, Dad."

"Should I?" said Norm's dad, the vein on the side of his head beginning to throb – a sure-fire sign that he was getting stressed. Not that Norm noticed. "Sorry, Norman. I'll try and be more specific next time."

"Thanks," said Norm.

Father and son looked at each other for a moment.

"So?" said Norm's dad.

"So?" said Norm.

"Off you go!"

"But..."

"But, what?" said Norm's dad, getting more and more exasperated.

48

"I'm supposed to be tidying my room," said Norm.

"Well, that'll just have to wait then, won't it, Norman?"

Norm grinned. "Oh, all right then, Dad. If you insist."

CHAPTER 5

Normally, Norm would have cycled to the allotments and been there and back in a few minutes. Today, however, was shaping up to be anything *but* normal. Norm wasn't actually *allowed* on his bike. On the one hand, Norm found this intensely infuriating and frustrating. On the other hand though, it did at least mean that Norm had to *walk* to the allotments – therefore taking much longer, and *therefore* delaying the fateful moment when he finally had to start tidying his room. In a funny kind of way, slipping up and hurting his wrist had actually been a bit of a blessing.

Even so, it felt very weird to Norm passing places and things that were usually no more than blurs because he zoomed past them so quickly. Why anyone *ever* walked anywhere when there was a faster alternative was a complete mystery to Norm.

Walking, as far as Norm was concerned, was quite literally a waste of time. As well as very annoying. What was even **more** annoying was the fact that when he **eventually** got to the allotments, Grandpa was nowhere to be seen. Not unless he was inside his shed. And judging by the size of the padlock on the door of the shed, he wasn't. Not unless Grandpa had suddenly taken up escapology. And as far as Norm knew, he hadn't.

Gordon flipping Bennet! thought Norm. All that walking for nothing? What was he supposed to do now? Actually wait or something? Norm didn't **do** waiting. Waiting was even more of a waste of time than walking. Grandpa could be **anywhere**! He might not even be planning to **come** to the allotments today! Norm could still be waiting this time next flipping week!

Norm sighed. If his dad wasn't such a flipping skinflint, he'd have given him money to actually

buy a cauliflower from the supermarket. That's if supermarkets even **did** own-brand flipping cauliflowers. It was **so** embarrassing, thought Norm. **Everything** had to be flipping supermarket-own-brand these days – from baked beans to flipping toilet roll. And as Norm knew only too well from bitter personal experience, there was **nothing** worse than supermarket-own-brand toilet roll.

There was only one thing for it, decided Norm. He was just going to have to take a cauliflower and tell Grandpa about it later. He knew that Grandpa wouldn't mind. He probably wouldn't even notice one was missing. Not unless he went round counting vegetables every day he wouldn't, anyway. And surely nobody was **that** sad!

Hmm, pondered Norm, squatting amongst the greenery. Which ones were cauliflowers? Everything looked the flipping same – all green and, well, vegetably. It wasn't something he'd ever had to think about before. Frankly, Norm could hardly believe he was thinking about it *now*.

"What do you think you're doing?" said a voice.

"AAAAAARGH!!!" screamed Norm, spinning round to see a stern-faced woman staring at him disapprovingly.

"Well?"

"It's not what it looks like," said Norm.

"Really?" said the woman. "Because it *looks* like you're stealing vegetables to me."

"Oh right," said Norm standing up. "I thought you thought I was having a –"

"So you're not denying it, then?"

"Not denying what?"

"That you were about to steal a cauliflower."

Norm was outraged. What did she think he was? Some kind of flipping vegeburglar? How flipping dare she?

"I'm **not** stealing!" said Norm indignantly. "I'm **borrowing**!"

"**Borrowing**?" said the woman doubtfully. "So you intend to bring them back, then?"

"It," said Norm.

"Pardon?" said the woman.

"I only want a cauliflower."

"Just one?"

Norm nodded. And he had no intention of bringing it back either. Bringing it **up**, possibly. But definitely not bringing it back.

"Is there a problem?" said Grandpa, walking up the path carrying a tin of paint.

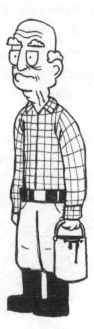

Norm breathed a huge sigh of relief. There was no such thing as a **bad** time to see Grandpa, but this was a particularly **good** time for him to suddenly turn up out of the blue. "Hi, Grandpa."

Grandpa looked at Norm and pulled a face. "*Grandpa*?"

The woman looked at Grandpa. "So...you don't know this child, then?"

Grandpa shook his head. "Never seen him before in my life."

"I knew it!" said the woman triumphantly.

"But..." said Norm.

Grandpa's eyes crinkled ever so slightly in the corners. It was the closest he ever came to smiling. "I'm kidding. Of **course** I know him."

"Oh," said the woman, looking and sounding somewhat crestfallen.

"Very funny, Grandpa," said Norm. "Very funny."

"I'm sorry, but it did look a bit suspicious," said the woman. "I was just being vigilant."

Gordon flipping Bennet! thought Norm. First he had to deal with Chelsea sticking her nose in where it wasn't wanted, and now Sherlock flipping Holmes here? Suddenly **everyone** was a flipping detective!

"Mmm, yes. Well, I suppose you can't be too careful," said Grandpa.

"I'll leave you to it, then," said the woman, heading off.

Grandpa watched her go before turning to Norm. "Would you like to explain what's going on?"

"I need a cauliflower," said Norm.

"Do you now?" said Grandpa.

"Well, *I* don't need one," said Norm. "But Mum does."

"I see," said Grandpa.

"I don't even *like* cauliflower."

"Neither do I."

"What?" said Norm. "You don't like cauliflower, Grandpa?"

"Not really, no," said Grandpa.

Norm pulled a face. "So...why do you grow them, then?"

Grandpa shrugged. "No idea. It's just something to do, I suppose."

Norm couldn't help laughing. "Do you like **anything** you grow?"

Grandpa thought for a moment. "Potatoes. I like potatoes. And I like peas."

"So you don't mind if I have one, then?"

"What?" said Grandpa. "Do I mind if you have a pea?"

"No," laughed Norm. "Do you mind if I have a **cauliflower**?"

"You can have the lot as far as I'm concerned."

58

Norm smiled. "Just the one, thanks, Grandpa."

Grandpa took a penknife out of his pocket, crouched down and cut through the stem of a cauliflower, before handing it to Norm.

"Eugh! It's gross!" said Norm. "It looks like a brain."

"Anything else I can do for you?" said Grandpa.

Norm puffed out his cheeks. "How long have you got?"

"Good question, Norman."

"What?" said Norm.

"Well, I mean, how long have **any** of us got?"

Norm was shocked. "You mean..."

"Exactly," said Grandpa. "None of us are going to be around forever."

Brilliant, thought Norm. Nothing like being reminded that we're all going to die to cheer you up. And he'd only come for a flipping cauliflower!

"How are you going to carry it, by the way?" said Grandpa.

"Uh?" said Norm.

"The cauliflower. On your bike," said Grandpa. "It's going to be a bit awkward, isn't it?"

"Oh, right," said Norm. "I've not come on my bike, Grandpa."

Grandpa looked at Norm as if Norm had just announced he'd been a badger in a previous life.

"You've not come on your bike?"

Norm shook his head.

"Why?"

"Long story, Grandpa. Some other time, maybe. I really ought to get going."

"Yes," said Grandpa. "You really ought to."

"What do you mean?" said Norm.

"Well, unless you want to help me paint the shed?"

That did the trick. Norm was off down the path like a shot. Even **without** his bike.

CHAPTER 6

Norm soon slowed down once he was clear of the allotments. He was still in no great hurry to get home. Or any kind of hurry for that matter. Which was why, instead of taking the direct route, Norm chose to go the slightly longer way instead.

As he trudged along, carrying the cauliflower, Norm began to replay the conversation he'd just had with Grandpa in his head. Having a conversation with Grandpa, thought Norm, could be a bit like a journey in itself. Sometimes it took an unexpected detour. But Norm liked that. He didn't mind never knowing what Grandpa was going to come out with next, and just blurting out whatever happened to be on his mind at the time.

"Gordon flipping Bennet!" said Norm as a bike suddenly whizzed past, only narrowly avoiding hitting him.

"OI! WATCH WHERE YOU'RE GOING, YOU MUPPET!"

What? thought Norm. There he was, walking along, minding his own business and some random nutjob tells *him* to watch where he's going? Honestly! What a flipping cheek! *Norm* wasn't the one riding his bike along the pavement like a flipping maniac!

Norm squinted into the distance to see if he could recognise whoever it was. But it was too late. All Norm could make out was that whoever it was, was wearing purple. It wasn't a lot to go on.

"Hope they get a flipping puncture," he muttered.

Norm sighed. The truth was that he was insanely jealous. He wished that he *was* the one riding his bike along the pavement like a maniac. He would have liked nothing **better** than to be riding his bike along the pavement like a maniac. What was he doing instead? Walking along it like a right doughnut, carrying a cauli-flipping-flower! It just wasn't fair, thought Norm. It just wasn't flipping fair at all.

"Well, well, well," said a voice when Norm turned into the precinct a few minutes later.

Looking up, Norm could see a boy on a bike ahead of him. More significantly, the boy was wearing a purple hoodie.

"Is it a bird? Is it a plane? No – it's Cauliflower Boy!"

Brilliant, thought Norm. Just what he needed. A flipping comedian.

"So what's your superpower, Cauliflower Boy? Producing wind?"

Norm sighed. What exactly was this guy's problem? Was he like this to **everyone** – or did Norm just happen to be in the right place at the right time? Or the **wrong** place at the **wrong** time, depending on which way you looked at it. Either way, Norm's gut reaction was to say something. Something so witty and cutting that the boy in the purple hoodie would deflate like a leaky space hopper. But what? wondered Norm. He couldn't think of **anything** to say – let alone anything witty, or cutting. It was **so** flipping annoying. What was even **more** annoying was that Norm just **knew** he'd think of something later on. Something that he'd wish he'd said at the time. But it would it too flipping late by then, wouldn't it? Unless he found out the guy's number and texted him, or left him a message on Facebook. And how was he supposed to do **that**?

"Is he bothering you?" said a voice.

Norm spun round to see a girl walking towards him, carrying a couple of bags of shopping. He couldn't help staring. Not only did the girl have long, jet black hair, she was also **dressed** entirely in black and was wearing big, black, clumpy boots. In direct contrast, her face was whiter than any other face Norm had ever seen before. Ghostly white, almost. Unnaturally white, in fact, thought Norm. Like a snowman. Or **snowgirl**, anyway.

"Erm…"

"What are **you** doing here, Alice?" sneered the boy in the purple hoodie. "I thought you only came out at night."

"Shut it, Zak!" spat the girl.

Zak? thought Norm. He used to know someone called Zak, didn't he? But that was a **long** time ago…

"I know you, don't I?" said the girl.

"Who? Me?" said Norm.

"Well, I already know **him**," said the girl with a tilt of her head. "Unfortunately."

"Ha, ha," said Zak sarcastically.

"Norman, isn't it?"

"Er, yeah," said Norm.

"Alice?" said the girl. "Alice Knight?"

"Aka **Dark** Alice," said Zak.

Alice shot Zak a withering look. "You'll have to excuse my brother. He thinks he's funny."

"Yeah, well, at least I don't walk round holding a cauliflower," snapped Zak.

"You remember Norman, don't you, Zak?" said Alice.

"Nah," said Zak. "Never seen him before in my life."

"Course you do, you muppet," said Alice. "He used to live next **door**!"

What? thought Norm as the penny finally dropped. **This** was the same Zak that he used to know? Zak flipping **Knight**? Whoa! **He'd** certainly changed! Well, obviously he'd changed. The last time Norm had seen him must have been when he was about six, running round dressed as Batman or something. Now here he was, acting all cool, like he was the bee's flipping knees!

"You were in the same **class**!" said Alice. "**Surely** you remember?"

Zak shrugged. "Nah."

"He was only little when we moved," said Alice, turning back to Norm.

Norm nodded. "So, have you..."

"Moved back?" said Alice. "Yeah. Not to the same house though."

"Right," said Norm. "We've moved as well."

"Cool," said Alice. "Which way are you going?"

"Erm, that way," said Norm, pointing ahead.

"Me too," said Alice. "Mind if I come with you?"

Norm shrugged. "If you want."

"Let's go."

Alice started walking straight towards her brother.

"Shift," she said.

"What do you say?" said Zak.

"*Now*," said Alice.

Zak reluctantly did as he was told and pushed himself back slightly on his bike so that his sister could pass.

Alice stopped and turned round. "You coming, or what?"

"Er, yeah," said Norm, setting off.

"Norman," muttered Zak as Norm brushed past. "What kind of name's *that*?"

"I've got the drinks, Za—" said a voice, before suddenly trailing off.

Norm spun round to see someone coming out of the supermarket carrying two cans of Coke. Someone he really hadn't expected to see. Certainly not here anyway. And definitely not now.

"Hi, Norm," said Mikey.

"Hi, Mikey," said Norm.

CHAPTER 7

The rest of the journey home was a bit of a blur as far as Norm was concerned. Bumping into Mikey at the precinct had come as one heck of a shock. Norm still couldn't quite believe it had actually happened. It was almost as if his visit to the allotments had been a dream. The only reason he knew it **wasn't** a dream was because of the disgusting smell of boiling cauliflower wafting up the stairs from the kitchen. At least Norm **presumed** it was the smell of cauliflower. Either that or John had been sick again. It was hard to tell the difference, frankly.

As Norm lay on his bed, staring up at the ceiling, the implications of what he'd just witnessed slowly began to sink in. As far as he could tell, the moment Mikey had found out that **Norm** couldn't go biking with him, he'd gone straight out and found someone **else** to go biking with instead. Never mind the fact that the **reason** Norm couldn't go biking was because he'd hurt himself! It was almost as if Mikey wasn't actually **bothered** about Norm and what had happened to him.

Norm flexed his wrist. It hardly hurt at all now. In fact, the **only** thing that hurt was Norm's feelings. How could Mikey do this to him? Mikey was **his** best friend – not Zak flipping Knight's! Who did this guy think he *was* – turning up out of the blue, thinking he was flipping **it**? And how come he'd suddenly hooked up with Mikey anyway? It was **so** annoying!

What was even **more** annoying, thought Norm, was that none of this would have happened if he hadn't slipped in the sick in the first place. Stupid flipping dog.

"Lunchtime," said Dave.

"Gordon flipping Bennet!" yelled Norm, looking round to see his youngest brother standing by his bed.

"Language," said Dave.

"Well, you might have knocked first," said Norm.

Dave pulled a face. "Why?"

"Why?" said Norm.

Dave nodded.

"Because...because..."

"Because what?" said Dave.

"Just *because*, Dave! All right?"

Dave thought for a moment. "That's not a proper reason."

Norm sighed. He wasn't in the mood for this. Not that he ever *was*. But now, it had to be said, was an *especially* bad time.

"Anything else?"

"Yeah," said Dave.

"What?" said Norm.

"Mum wants to know if you've tidied your room yet."

Norm was doing his best to keep calm. "Does it **look** like I've tidied my room yet, Dave?"

Dave looked around. "Er, no. Not really."

"Well then," said Norm. "There's your answer."

"'Kay," said Dave.

"Anything **else**?" said Norm.

"I'll do it."

"What?" said Norm.

"I'll tidy your room for you," said Dave. "If you want."

Norm studied Dave for a moment, expecting him to burst out laughing any second – or at least crack a smile. Surely there was a catch. In Norm's experience there usually was.

"Why are you looking at me like that?" said Dave.

"Dunno," said Norm. "Just am."

"Oh, I geddit," said Dave. "You think I'm going to ask for something in return, or make some kind of deal, right?"

"No!" said Norm, like this was the furthest thing from his mind. "How could you even *think* that, Dave?"

"Really?" said Dave.

"Of course."

"Sorry."

"That's OK," said Norm. "But now you come to mention it..."

"I knew it!" said Dave triumphantly.

"Well?" said Norm.

"I don't want **anything** in return," said Dave. "Consider it an act of brotherly love."

Norm pulled a face. "Are you feeling all right?"

"Perfectly all right, thank you," said Dave.

Norm wasn't sure that **he** was feeling all right. One of his brothers committing a random act of kindness? On a list of

NORM'S LIST OF UNLIKELY THINGS TO HAPPEN
- I become Prime Minister
- DAVE/BRIAN committing a random act of kindness
- Grandpa getting into hip-hop
-
-
-

'Unlikely Things to Happen' this came somewhere just above Grandpa getting into hip-hop and somewhere just below Norm becoming Prime Minister. But Norm wasn't about to look a gift horse in the mouth, or whatever that expression was. And whatever a flipping gift horse was, when it was at home!

"Thanks, Dave," said Norm, hopping off the bed and heading for the door.

"Don't mention it," said Dave.

CHAPTER 8

"What's for lunch, Mum?" said Norm, sitting down at the table.

"You'll get what you're given," said Norm's dad.

"Uh?" said Norm.

"I said, you'll get what you're given," said Norm's dad. "This isn't a restaurant you know."

Good job, thought Norm. Be a pretty flipping rubbish one if it was.

"Have you washed your hands, by the way?" said Norm's dad. "I mean **recently**. Not **ever**."

"*I* have, Dad," said Brian, grinning mischievously at Norm.

"Creep," muttered Norm.

"Cauliflower cheese," said Norm's mum, plonking a plate down in front of Norm.

There were *some* things, thought Norm, that just **didn't** belong together on the same plate. **Cauliflower** and **cheese** were two of them. Frankly, thought Norm, cauliflower and cheese didn't belong in the same postcode – let alone on the same flipping plate. Then again, in Norm's opinion, the only place cauliflower belonged was in the bin. He'd hated it before, but after recent events he abso-flipping-lutely **loathed** it now.

FROM RH1   FROM SN2

"Penny for your thoughts, love?"

"What?" said Norm distractedly.

"Penny for your thoughts?"

"Make it a quid and you've got yourself a deal," said Norm.

"What did you say?" said Norm's dad, the vein on the side of his head beginning to throb.

"Nothing, Dad."

"Where's Dave?" said Norm's mum.

But before anyone could answer, there was a knock at the front door.

"I'll get it!" said Norm, jumping up, only too happy to avoid questions about what Dave might be doing. And even **happier** to avoid the cauliflower cheese.

It didn't occur to Norm to wonder who it might actually **be**. If it had, he might not have been **quite** so keen to leave the table.

"Oh, it's you," said Norm, opening the door.

"Hi, Norm," said Mikey sheepishly. "I just wanted to..."

"It's OK, Mikey," said Norm, interjecting. "You don't need to explain."

Mikey looked surprised. "Really?"

Norm shrugged. "Course not. Why should you?"

"Erm, right," said Mikey. "I just thought you might be..."

"No, really, Mikey," said Norm. "You can hang round with whoever you like. Doesn't bother *me*."

"It's only because you called to say you couldn't come out."

"Mikey?"

"Yeah?"

"It's fine," said Norm.

But despite Norm's reassurances, Mikey **still** looked uncomfortable. As if he'd got something he needed to get off his chest.

"Can I say something, Norm?"

Norm shrugged. "I dunno, Mikey. Can you?"

"He found me."

"What?" said Norm. "Who did?"

"Zak Knight."

"Oh, right," said Norm. "What do you mean he found you? **Where** did he find you?"

"On Facebook," said Mikey.

"Facebook?" said Norm.

Mikey nodded. "He said he remembered me from when he used to live here."

What? thought Norm. So Zak Knight had remembered **Mikey**, but not **him**? Flipping typical. And also, how flipping come? What was it about **Mikey** that was so memorable? What had **Mikey** got that **he** hadn't?

"I didn't get in touch with **him**, Norm! **He** got in touch with *me*!"

Norm sighed. "Yeah, whatever, Mikey."

"It doesn't mean…"

"Mikey?" said Norm.

"Yeah?"

"I said, **whatever**."

"Hi, Mikey," said Dave, appearing at the foot of the stairs.

"Oh, hi, Dave," said Mikey.

"That was quick," said Norm to Dave.

"What was?" said Mikey.

"Tidying my room," said Norm.

Mikey looked puzzled. "You got your little brother to tidy your room?"

"I don't mind," said Dave. "I offered!"

"I wish *I* had a brother," said Mikey.

"You're welcome to him," said Norm. "No offence, Dave."

"None taken," said Dave.

Mikey's phone rang. He took it out of his pocket to see who it was.

"Aren't you going to answer it?" asked Dave.

"Nah," said Mikey, putting the phone back in his pocket.

"Why not?" said Dave.

"Erm…" said Mikey.

Norm had a pretty good idea why Mikey was reluctant to answer the phone.

"It's him, isn't it?"

"What?" said Mikey.

"Zak Knight?"

Mikey didn't answer. He didn't **need** to.

"Who is it, love?" called Norm's mum from the kitchen.

"Nobody, Mum," said Norm, closing the door.

CHAPTER 9

"Nice of you to join us, Dave," said Norm's dad as Norm and Dave sat down at the table.

"No problem, Dad," said Dave cheerfully.

"I think Dad's being sarcastic, Dave," said Brian out of the corner of his mouth.

Dave pulled a face. "Isn't sarcasm supposed to be the lowest form of humour?"

"Just eat up, Dave, there's a good boy," said Norm's mum quickly. "It's your favourite!"

"Mmmm," said Dave, tucking in enthusiastically.

Norm looked at Dave in sheer disbelief. How could cauliflower cheese possibly be ***anyone's*** favourite? It was at times like this that Norm seriously doubted whether he really **was** biologically related to his brothers – or whether in fact there'd been some kind of mix-up at the hospital.

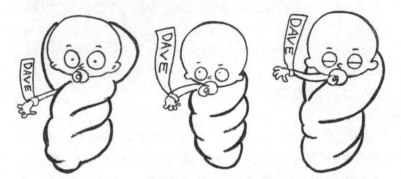

"Who's Zak Knight?" said Dave, between mouthfuls.

"Doesn't matter," said Norm quickly.

Norm's mum and dad exchanged glances.

"Why doesn't it matter?" said Brian.

"It just flipping doesn't, all right?" said Norm.

"Language," said Dave.

"Shut up, Dave," said Norm.

"Well, this is nice," said Norm's dad.

Dave pulled a face. "Why?"

"I think Dad's being sarcastic again," said Brian out of the corner of his mouth.

"Why?" said Dave.

Gordon flipping Bennet, thought Norm. Much more of this and he was going to have to make his excuses and leave the table – whether he'd finished the cauliflower cheese or not. Preferably not.

"The Knights used to be our neighbours," said Norm's mum.

"What, you mean when we lived in our old house?" said Dave.

Norm's mum nodded. "They left when you were born."

"Don't flipping blame them," muttered Norm. "Wish I had."

"What?" said Dave.

Norm's mum smiled. "**When** you were born, Dave. Not **because** you were born."

"Right," said Dave. "Why?"

It was a good question, actually, thought Norm. Why **did** Zak Knight move? Did **his** dad get sacked for gambling at work and blowing all the family savings, too? Had **he** had to move to a stupid little house with paper-thin walls and been forced to eat supermarket-own-brand flipping coco pops ever since as well?

"Why?" persisted Dave.

Norm's dad looked a bit uneasy. "Erm, well…"

"How's John, Brian?" said Norm's mum breezily, clearly wishing to change the subject.

"A lot better," said Brian.

"How do you **know**?" said Norm. "Have you asked him?"

"Don't be silly, Norman," said Brian.

"Oh yeah, I forgot," said Norm. "You don't speak Polish, do you, Brian?"

"Why didn't you ask Mikey in?" said Dave.

Norm glared at his little brother. "I just didn't, all right?"

"That's not a proper reason," said Dave.

"So that was **Mikey** at the door then?" said Norm's mum.

Norm nodded.

"Why did you say it was nobody then?"

Norm shrugged. "Dunno. Just did."

"That's not a proper..."

"Shut up, Dave, you little freak!"

snapped Norm.

"Well, there's nothing like a nice, friendly family meal," said Norm's dad.

Yeah, thought Norm. And this was **nothing** like a nice, friendly family meal. But that wasn't *his* flipping fault, was it? It wasn't **him** asking all the flipping questions! He just wanted to eat up as quickly as possible and go.

Norm looked up and saw that his mum was staring at him.

"What?"

"Is everything OK, love?"

"Yeah," said Norm. "Everything's fine, Mum."

Norm's mum raised her eyebrows. "Sure?"

Gordon flipping Bennet! thought Norm. Why couldn't his mum just drop the subject?

"You and Mikey haven't..."

Norm sighed. "Which part of 'fine' do you not understand?"

"Don't you **dare** talk to your mother like that, Norman!" said Norm's dad.

"But..."

"No buts, Norman! I'm warning you! One more word and you're out!"

Really? thought Norm. Just one more word? **Any** word?

"Right, that's it!" said Norm's dad. "Out!"

With pleasure, thought Norm, getting up and heading for the door. With abso-flipping-lute pleasure.

CHAPTER 10

Freed from the need to make stupid conversation and answer even **stupider** questions, Norm headed gratefully for the garage. If he couldn't actually **ride** his bike, he could at least fiddle about and tinker with it. Of course, when he was World Mountain Biking Champion, he'd have a whole team of people to do that kind of thing *for* him – personal mechanics and the like – but until that actually happened, Norm would have to do it for himself. Or at least **try** to.

Norm opened the door, immediately flooding the interior of the garage with bright sunlight. There in the middle – propped up against a sofa they could no longer find room for – was Norm's pride and joy. His one true love. His bike.

"My precious," said Norm in a funny voice. What was that slimy little alien guy called again? The one in *Lord of the Rings* that looked a bit like E.T.? Brian would know, thought Norm. Brian was **such** a flipping geek.

"Talking to yourself again, **Norman**?" said a voice from the other side of the fence.

Gordon flipping Bennet! thought Norm, without bothering to turn round. Did Chelsea **really** have to come outside every time that **he** did? It was like she was keeping a flipping lookout from her house or something! Like a spider waiting for a fly to land on its web. The slightest vibration and she was out like a flipping shot. Didn't she have anything **better** to do? Apparently not.

"It **is** you, isn't it, **Norman**?" said Chelsea. "I hardly recognised you without your PJs on."

Norm could feel himself going bright red. He couldn't help it. It was **SO** flipping annoying.

"What do you want?"

"Oh, I'm fine, thanks," said Chelsea. "How are you?"

"Busy," said Norm.

"Doing what?"

"Stuff," said Norm.

"Stuff?" said Chelsea.

Norm nodded.

"What kind of stuff?"

"Just, you know...stuff," said Norm.

"Right, I see," said Chelsea, as if that somehow explained everything. "How's the dog?"

Norm shrugged. "Dunno."

"Really?"

"Really," said Norm.

"Don't you care?" said Chelsea.

Norm shrugged again. "Not really."

"Really?" said Chelsea.

"Yeah, really," said Norm. "It's just a flipping dog."

"I don't believe you."

"What?" said Norm. "You don't believe it's just a dog?"

"Now, now, **Norman**," said Chelsea. "You know perfectly well what I mean."

Norm sighed. He wasn't sure how much more of this he could take. Why couldn't she just leave him in peace? Maybe if he started fiddling about with his bike again she'd get the hint and go.

"What are you doing?" said Chelsea, neither getting the hint nor going as Norm took a can of oil from a shelf and squirted a bit on the chain.

"What does it flipping *look* like?"

snapped Norm.

"All right, **Norman**! Keep your hair on!" said Chelsea.

"Norman?"

Norm spun round to see a guy on a bike at the end of the drive. He looked kind of familiar. Like a bigger version of someone else. But who? wondered Norm. Who did this guy remind him of?

"Alice said she'd seen you."

Of **course**, thought Norm. **That's** who he was! Zak Knight's big brother! What was his name again?

"I'm Chelsea," said Chelsea.

"Hal," said the guy.

That was it, thought Norm. Hal. Hal Knight. So Chelsea **did** have her uses after all!

Flutter Flutter

"Pleased to meet you," said Chelsea.

"Yeah, you must be," grinned Hal.

Norm couldn't help laughing.

"What's up with you?" said Chelsea.

"Nothing," said Norm.

"So **you** moved too, huh?" said Hal.

"Yeah. Worse flipping luck," said Norm.

"Why's that then?" said Hal.

Norm sighed. "Long story."

"Right," said Hal. "So how old are you now?"

"Nearly thirteen," said Norm.

"Whoa," said Hal. "Last time I saw you, you must've been about six!"

Chelsea laughed.

"What's so funny about that?" said Norm.

"Nothing," said Chelsea. "I just can't imagine you being six, that's all, *Norman*."

Norm glared at his occasional next door neighbour. *He* couldn't imagine *her* being anything other than incredibly annoying.

"How old are *you*, Hal?" asked Chelsea.

"Seventeen," said Hal.

"Really?" said Chelsea.

"Well, *nearly* seventeen anyway," said Hal. "Nice bike by the way, Norman."

"What?" said Norm distractedly. "Oh, right. Thanks. You too."

"Thanks," said Hal. "I'd really like to get a new one but I haven't got any money."

Tell me about it, thought Norm. Not only could he *relate* to Hal, he was beginning to *like* him too. He seemed a lot nicer than his *brother*, anyway.

"Where do you go?" said Hal.

"What?" said Norm.

"Biking?" said Hal.

"Oh, right," said Norm. "The woods?"

"Yeah," said Hal. "Some really cool trails up there."

"Yeah," said Norm.

"Fancy going?"

"What, you mean now?" said Norm.

Hal shrugged. "Why not?"

"Can't," said Norm.

"Aw, won't Mummy let you?" grinned Chelsea.

"Very funny," said Norm.

"So why can't you then?" said Hal.

"Long story," said Norm.

"*Another* long story?"
said Chelsea.
"Honestly, *Norman*,
you should write
a book!"

Yeah, thought Norm.
And Chelsea should

keep her flipping nose out of it and clear off.

"Oh well," said Hal, beginning to pedal away. "Stuff to do."

"Yeah, me too," said Norm, watching him go.

"Stuff?" said Chelsea.

Gordon flipping Bennet! thought Norm. Here we go again.

CHAPTER 11

There were a great many things that weren't Norm's fault. Well, as far as Norm was concerned there were, anyway. His dad getting sacked and them all having to move to a stupid little house and only eat own-brand coco pops, for instance. That **definitely** wasn't his fault. Neither was the fact that the only place Norm could get decent Wi-Fi for his iPad was sitting on the toilet.

"What are you doing in there, Norman?" yelled Norm's dad from the other side of the door.

Norm sighed. What did his dad **think** he was flipping doing? He was on flipping Facebook!

"Won't be long, Dad!" yelled Norm.

"Correct!" yelled Norm's dad. "You **won't** be long!"

His dad really should be a comedian, thought Norm. And anyway, it wasn't **his** fault they only had one toilet these days, was it?

"Seriously, Norman. If you're not out in two minutes, I'll…I'll…I'll…"

Norm chuckled to himself as he imagined what his dad **might** do if he wasn't out of the toilet in two minutes. But Norm's amusement – as it so often was these days – was only short lived. He'd just read something on Facebook. Something he wished he **hadn't** read. Something that had only just been posted.

What? thought Norm. No way! Surely not? But…

Norm read the post again. Not that it made any difference. It still said **exactly** the same thing the second time round. Mikey had been asked for a sleepover. By Zak Knight. Zak **flipping** Knight. That was ridiculous. They didn't even **know** each other! They were practically strangers! What was going on? You didn't just meet someone and then two seconds later ask them for a flipping sleepover! And that was another thing, thought Norm. A **sleepover**? What were they? Nine-year-old **girls** or something?

Norm sighed and read the post for a **third** time. A whole bunch of different emotions were tumbling round his stomach, like clothes in a washing machine. It was hardly surprising. He and Mikey had been best friends forever. Well, not actually **forever** obviously, but a long time anyway. Since they were babies – and that was at least twelve years ago. Sure, there'd been ups and downs in that time. It would be weird if there **hadn't** been. But this? thought Norm. This wasn't so much a **down** as going over the edge of a flipping waterfall! Without a flipping boat!

Deep inside, of course, Norm **knew** that he was being unreasonable. He knew that he had no control over Mikey. He knew that Mikey could do whatever he wanted – **with** whoever he wanted to do it with. But even so, it was pretty hard to take.

Norm tried not to think about it. But the more he tried **not** to think about it, the more he actually thought about it. And the more he actually **thought** about it, the worse he actually felt. How could Mikey **do** this to him? **How**?

"You still in there?" yelled Norm's dad.

Norm was so fed up that he couldn't even be bothered to come up with a sarcastic reply. "Coming, Dad."

Norm's dad sounded surprised. "Pardon?"

"Just coming," said Norm, getting up, opening the door and coming face to face with his father.

"Have you washed your hands, Norman?"

"Didn't need to, Dad."

"What do you mean you didn't **need** to?"

Norm shrugged. "I didn't need to."

"Did you flush?" said Norm's dad, the vein on the

side of his head beginning to throb. Not that Norm noticed.

"I didn't **need** to," said Norm. "I didn't actually...you know..."

"What?"

yelled Norm.

"Don't take that attitude with me, young man!" said Norm's dad.

Uh? thought Norm. Attitude? What flipping attitude?

Norm's dad regarded Norm for a moment. "Are you OK?"

Was he OK? thought Norm. Course he wasn't OK! He'd never felt **less** OK in his life!

"Are you constipated?"

"No, Dad!"

Norm's dad pulled a face. "So what's the problem then?"

Norm sighed. "If you must know, I've just seen something on Facebook."

"What?" said Norm's dad, only noticing **now** that Norm had his iPad tucked under his arm. "That's disgusting!"

"Facebook's not disgusting, Dad!"

"No, but being **on** Facebook on the **toilet** is disgusting."

"But..."

"But what, Norman?"

"I wasn't **on** the toilet!" said Norm. "Well I mean, I was **on** the toilet – but

I wasn't actually **on** the toilet, if you see what I mean?"

"No, I don't, actually," said Norm's dad.

Luckily, Norm was spared from going into any more detail by a sudden shout from the direction of his bedroom.

"Norman?"

"Yes, Mum?"

"Bedroom! Now!"

Gordon flipping Bennet, thought Norm, heading off. If it wasn't one flipping thing it was another.

CHAPTER 12

"What?" said Norm, walking into his room.

"What?" said Norm's mum. "What do you **mean**, 'what'?"

"Uh, what?" said Norm.

Norm's mum sighed. "I said, what do you **mean**, 'what'?"

"I mean, what do you **want**, Mum?"

"What do I **want**?" said Norm's mum. "Is this some kind of joke, love?"

Joke? thought Norm. If it was then it wasn't very funny.

"What do you call this?" said Norm's mum.

Uh? thought Norm. This was getting weirder and weirder. What did he call **what**? What was his mum on about now? If only he could rewind the conversation and start again.

"What, Mum?"

"This," said Norm's mum, pointing at the bed.

Norm pulled a face. Was this some kind of trick question?

"Well?" said Norm's mum expectantly.

"Erm...a bed?" said Norm uncertainly.

"No, love!" said Norm's mum, beginning to sound exasperated. "***Under*** the bed!"

"Oh, right," said Norm. "Erm..."

"Is that your idea of tidying up? Just shoving stuff out of sight where no one can see it?"

Norm hadn't noticed when he'd fetched his iPad. But now that his mum mentioned it, it appeared that that was **precisely** what Dave had done. Just bunged everything under his bed instead of putting it away properly. How flipping annoying! Norm could have done *that* himself!

"It's not *my* fault," muttered Norm.

"Sorry?" said Norm's mum. "Whose fault **is** it, then?"

"Erm…" said Norm.

Norm's mum looked at Norm for a moment. "Come here, love," she said, sitting down on the bed and patting the space beside her.

"Do I **have** to, Mum?"

"Not if you really don't want to."

Norm not only really didn't want to, he really, **really** didn't want to. OK, so being summonsed to sit next to his mum was preferable to being summonsed to go and see his head teacher. But only just. Being summonsed to sit next to his mum inevitably meant Norm being probed and interrogated and asked about his flipping feelings and stuff. And Norm didn't **do** feelings. Feelings were a foreign country. One that Norm had no intention of ever visiting.

"Well?" said Norm's mum, patting the bed again.

Norm thought for a second. Perhaps this time it would be different. Perhaps this time his mum wanted to talk about something other than feelings.

Norm sat down.

"How are you *feeling*, love?" said Norm's mum gently. "Is something wrong?"

thought Norm. So much for *that* flipping theory then!

"There is, isn't there?"

"I'm *fine*, Mum," said Norm.

"Sure?"

"Sure, Mum."

"You're not *really* though, are you, love?" said Norm's mum. "I can tell."

How could his mum tell? wondered Norm. What was she? Flipping **psychic**, or something? It was **so** annoying!

"Do you want to talk about it?"

"No, Mum!" said Norm. "I **don't** want to talk about it, actually!"

"Ah," said Norm's mum. "So there **is** something wrong then?"

Norm sighed. His mum had set the trap and he'd fallen for it hook, line and flipping sinker. What a doughnut.

"What is it?" said Norm's mum.

Hang on a sec, thought Norm. Just because he'd fallen for it, didn't mean he had to tell the truth, did it? Not the **whole** truth anyway.

"Erm, well..."

"What, love?"

"I'm just a bit fed up I can't go biking, that's all."

"Oh, I **see**," said Norm's mum, sounding quite relieved. "So **that's** what it is."

Norm nodded.

"I thought it was something..."

"What?" said Norm.

"Well, something more..."

"What?" said Norm again.

"Serious," said Norm's mum. "Not that that's **not** serious, of course, love. I know how much you like your biking."

Norm nodded again. "Yeah."

"It's for the best though."

"What is?"

"That you don't go biking."

"Oh, right, yeah," said Norm, just glad that he'd managed to avoid having to tell his mum the **real** reason he was fed up.

"Not today, anyway," said Norm's mum. "We'll see how it is tomorrow."

Norm pulled a face. "See how **what** is?"

"Your wrist."

Norm hesitated ever so slightly. "Oh, right, yeah. My wrist."

"How is it?"

"It's OK."

"Which one was it again?"

Good question, thought Norm. Which one was it again? He had a 50/50 chance of getting it right.

"The right one?" said Norm.

Norm's mum laughed. "You don't sound very sure, love!"

"What?" said Norm. "No, definitely the right one, Mum."

"Poor baby," said Norm's mum.

"Muuuum!" said Norm. "I'm not a flipping baby!"

"You'll always be *my* baby, Norman."

Norm sighed. He **hated** it when his mum got all soppy. But he had to admit, **anything** was better than talking about his flipping feelings.

"Nothing else?"

Norm pulled a face. "What do you mean, Mum?"

"I mean is anything **else** wrong, love?"

Gordon flipping Bennet! thought Norm. Just when he thought he'd got away with it, his mum seemed determined to wheedle it out of him **somehow**.

"Er, don't think so, no," said Norm.

"Sure?"

"Sure," said Norm.

Norm's mum looked at Norm for a moment. "It's just that..."

"What?" said Norm.

"Well, you went a bit quiet when Dave mentioned Zak Knight earlier."

"Did I?" said Norm, trying to sound as casual as possible. "Don't remember that, Mum."

"Well, you did, love."

Norm shrugged. "Well, I didn't **mean** to."

Hmmm, said Norm's mum.

Norm **hated** it when his mum went **hmmm**. Even more than he hated it when she got all soppy!

What did **hmmm** even mean? It wasn't even a **proper** flipping word! It was **so** flipping annoying! One thing was for sure, thought Norm. It was time to change the subject.

"Mum?" said Norm.

"What, love?"

"I was just wondering…"

Norm's mum raised her eyebrows in anticipation.

"Can Mikey come for a sleepover tonight?"

CHAPTER 13

There was only **one** person more surprised than Norm's mum when Norm suddenly asked if Mikey could come for a sleepover – and that was Norm himself. Norm hadn't **meant** to ask. He had no idea he was **going** to ask until he actually did it. But rather like an accidental fart, it had just slipped out without warning. Unlike an accidental fart however, the after-effects were potentially much longer lasting. It wasn't simply a question of opening a window and hoping that it would disappear.

PARP

Norm had been surprised by quite how quickly his mum had agreed. Like she hadn't even had to think about it. Then again, thought Norm, his mum had always liked Mikey – mainly because he ate pretty much anything that was put in front of him. Unlike Norm, whose idea of getting his five a day was by eating an entire packet of fruit-flavoured chews.

Norm knew there'd be a catch, of course. There always flipping was. His mum couldn't **possibly** just say yes, could she? That would be **much** too straightforward. No, there were **bound** to be terms and flipping conditions like there were at the end of adverts on the radio or the telly, when some doughnut starts banging on about always reading the flipping label and how your life was at risk if you didn't keep up repayments or whatever. Sure enough there *was* a catch. Norm's mum had insisted that if Mikey was to come for a sleepover then Norm had to tidy his room again. But **properly** this time. Not that Norm had actually tidied it the **last** time. Dave had. But his mum didn't know that – and wouldn't be terribly impressed if she found out, either. Naturally Norm had **tried** to argue, making the point that it wasn't really **worth** tidying his room, because if Mikey was coming for a sleepover it would only get all messed up again. His mum was having none of it though. Norm had to tidy his room, she'd said. Take it or leave it, she'd said. Norm took it. Which was how he came to have his head underneath his bed and his backside sticking up in the air when Grandpa suddenly appeared in the doorway.

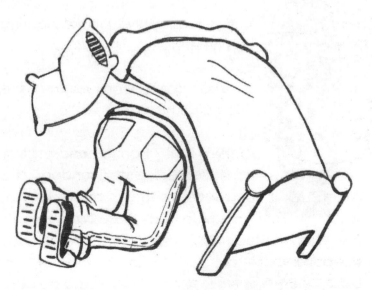

"I never forget a face," said Grandpa.

"Aaaaaaaagh!" screamed Norm, getting an almighty fright and bumping his head on the underside of the bed for the second time that day.

"Mind your head," said Grandpa.

"Very funny, Grandpa," said Norm, emerging from under the bed to see Grandpa splattered from head to foot in paint.

"I'm surprised you're not wearing a helmet."

"Uh?" said Norm, rubbing the back of his head.

"All that health and safety nonsense," said Grandpa. "It's a wonder they actually let kids outside at all these days."

Norm smiled.

"What have you lost?"

"Uh?" said Norm.

"What are you looking for?" said Grandpa. "Under the bed?"

"Oh, right. Nothing," said Norm.

Grandpa pulled a face. "You were looking for nothing?"

"I'm just tidying up."

"Tidying up?" said Grandpa, as if Norm had just announced that he was taking up knitting. "What for?"

Norm sighed. "Long story, Grandpa."

"I've got all day," said Grandpa.

"Really?" said Norm.

"Actually, no, I haven't," said Grandpa, looking at his watch. "I've got to get down to the bookie's."

Norm looked at Grandpa for a moment.

"What?" said Grandpa.

"You **do** know you're covered in paint, don't you?"

Grandpa immediately looked horrified. "What? Really? You're joking! Why didn't you say so before?"

For a split second Norm actually thought Grandpa was being serious, before noticing Grandpa's eyes crinkling ever so slightly in the corners.

"I knew you knew that," said Norm.

"Right," said Grandpa.

"I **did**!" protested Norm.

Grandpa raised a single, cloud-like eyebrow. "Really?"

Norm sighed. "OK. Not really."

"Kids today," said Grandpa.

Norm smiled. "You finished, then?"

"Finished what?" said Grandpa.

"Painting your shed."

"Yeah," said Grandpa. "No thanks to you."

"Yeah, well."

"Well what?"

"I've been busy."

"Hmm," said Grandpa, clearly not convinced. "Busy doing nothing more like."

"Yeah, well," said Norm.

"What's the use of a well without a bucket?"

"Uh?"

"Just something my mother used to say to me when I was your age," said Grandpa.

Norm couldn't imagine Grandpa *ever* being his age – let alone having a mother. So that would have been his what? Great-grandma? Norm was rubbish at working stuff like that out. And besides, there were more pressing matters to attend to right now. Like how he was going to go about asking Mikey for a sleepover at his house – *without* Mikey knowing that Norm already *knew* that he'd been asked for a sleepover at Zak flipping Knight's house!

"Right," said Grandpa, heading for the stairs. "Better get on, I suppose."

"Wait for me, Grandpa," said Norm, following. "I'll come with you."

"Where are you going, love?" said Norm's mum, standing in the hallway.

"Er, Mikey's," said Norm.

"What for?"

Norm shrugged. "Stuff."

"Hmm," said Norm's mum. "You finished tidying that room of yours yet?"

Norm grinned. "WIP, Mum."

"WIP?" said Norm's mum.

"Work in progress."

"Hmm," said Norm's mum again. "I'm not sure I should be letting you..."

"I'll take the dog for a walk if you like."

Norm's mum pulled a face. "Really?"

"Really," said Norm, going off to find John.

"Well, I suppose he *could* do with a walk, now you come to mention it. Thanks, love."

"See?" said Grandpa to Norm's mum. "He's not *all* bad."

CHAPTER 14

Norm, Grandpa and John walked together for a little while in the late-afternoon sunshine, chatting about this, that and the other. Well, at least Norm and Grandpa chatted about this, that and the other. John was more preoccupied with barking at cats and stopping every few seconds to pee on lampposts. Eventually, though, it was time for them to go their separate ways – Grandpa to the bookie's, Norm and John onwards towards Mikey's house.

Norm used to live quite close to Mikey's before they'd moved. Or rather, before they'd **had** to move and start eating own-brand coco pops. Not as close as he'd lived to Zak Knight's at one time – but pretty close all the same. Now, though, instead of it only taking **one** song on his iPod to bike to Mikey's, it could take as many as four or five songs, depending on how long the songs were and how fast Norm was going. Today, of course, it was going to take longer. Much longer.

Norm tried to recall what the Knights had been like as neighbours. The truth was, Norm's memories of those days were pretty hazy. But then, a lot of Norm's memories were pretty hazy – particularly when it came to remembering what homework he had and whether it was his turn to do the washing up or not. Surely there had to be **something** that had stuck in his mind after all this time, thought Norm. Had he and Zak ever played together? Had **Mikey** and Zak ever played together? What had Zak actually been **like** back then? It was quite hard to imagine, what with him being such a flipping doughnut **now**.

Norm knew he couldn't spend **too** long dwelling on the past. It was time to dwell on the present – and what he was going to say when he finally saw Mikey. He knew he was going to have to play it quite cool. He knew he couldn't afford to appear **too** desperate. In fact, the more Norm thought about it, the more he realised he was going to have to make it look like he'd asked Mikey for a sleepover as a spur of the moment thing. Like it had been the **last** thing on his mind. Not the **first**!

The closer Norm got to Mikey's, the more wound up and agitated he became. By the time he reached the end of Mikey's street, Norm felt like an over-pumped-up football. And any second now, he was going to burst.

Norm stopped and took a deep breath. He needed a moment to compose himself and gather his thoughts. Actually, thought Norm, he needed more than a moment. His thoughts were all over the flipping place, like sheep scattered in a field. What Norm *really* needed now was a dog, to herd them all together again. A proper dog. Not a rubbish one, like John.

Norm gradually began to feel light-headed, as if he was about to fall over. What was going on? he wondered, before eventually realising that he **still** hadn't breathed out again.

"Oh. Er, hi, Norm," said Mikey, stepping out of his front door, and looking **and** sounding as if Norm was the last person on earth he was hoping to see.

"Er, hi," said Norm.

"Hi, John," said Mikey.

WOOF! went John.

Mikey pulled a face. "You OK?"

"Yeah, I'm fine. Why?"

"You're very red," said Mikey.

Norm shrugged. "Forgot to breathe."

"What?" said Mikey.

"Doesn't matter," muttered Norm.

There was an awkward pause whilst Norm and Mikey looked at each other for a few seconds. Never mind being the best of friends, it was like they'd never even *met* before.

"So, er..." began Mikey at last.

"What?" said Norm.

"What brings you here?"

Norm shrugged again. "I was just passing."

"But..." said Mikey.

"What?" said Norm.

"We live in a cul-de-sac."

"Yeah? So?" said Norm.

"So you can't have just been passing."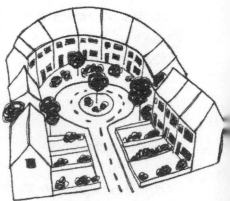

Gordon flipping Bennet, thought Norm. If he'd wanted to be quizzed and interrogated he could have stayed at home! "Maybe I wasn't then."

"Wasn't what?" said Mikey.

"Just passing," said Norm.

"Right," said Mikey.

There was another awkward pause.

"I was just wondering…"

"What?" said Mikey.

"Nothing," said Norm.

"No, go on, Norm. What were you wondering?"

"Doesn't matter."

Mikey looked at Norm. "Really?"

"Really," said Norm.

"I don't believe you."

Norm was quite taken aback. He wasn't used to Mikey standing up to him like this. Not that Norm was ever horrible or nasty to Mikey. But Norm was normally the one in charge. Well, not exactly in **charge**. But still, it just felt strange to Norm to hear Mikey say that he didn't believe him. It was almost like it was out of character. It just wasn't like Mikey at all.

"Well?" said Mikey expectantly.

"What's the use of a well without a bucket?" said Norm.

Mikey pulled a face. "What?"

"Doesn't matter," said Norm. "If you must know, I was going to…"

"What, Norm?" said Mikey.

Norm sighed. "Dunno. Ask if you fancied having a sleepover or something."

"Oh, I see," said Mikey hesitantly. "I'd love to, Norm, I really would…"

Norm sensed a **but** coming. And he was right.

"But…"

"But what?" said Norm.

"Well, you see, the thing is…"

"What, Mikey? What's the thing?"

Mikey seemed to be finding it difficult to look Norm in the eye. "Nothing."

"I'll tell you what the thing is, Cauliflower Boy," said Zak Knight, suddenly appearing in the doorway behind Mikey. "Mikey's already made other arrangements for tonight."

Norm wasn't merely gobsmacked, he was utterly stunned. Never mind feeling like an over-pumped-up football, for a split second Norm felt like he'd had every last bit of air sucked *out* of him. The possibility that Zak Knight might actually *be* at Mikey's house just hadn't occurred to him. Norm knew he ought to say *something*. Anything at all. It didn't matter what. As long as he didn't continue to stand there gawping like a flipping goldfish.

"Oh, yeah?" said Norm finally.

Zak Knight smirked. "Yeah. Isn't that right, Mikey?"

Norm turned to his friend. In fairness to Mikey, he did at least have the decency to look like he wished that the ground would open up and swallow him whole. He was clearly feeling very uncomfortable. Good, thought Norm. He flipping ought to be, too.

"Well, Mikey?" said Norm. "Have you?"

"What?" said Mikey.

"Made other arrangements?"

"Erm…" said Mikey.

It was all Norm needed to know. That **erm** told him more than a thousand proper words *ever* could.

"Hey, that's fine," said Norm as nonchalantly as possible. As if the thought of Mikey having a sleepover at Zak Knight's wasn't actually eating him up at all. As if he wasn't actually angry, or confused, or devastated. As if he didn't feel in the least bit abandoned. Or insanely jealous. Or completely and utterly betrayed. "No probs, Mikey."

Zak Knight chuckled quietly to himself.

"What?" said Norm. "You think I'm bothered? I'm not bothered."

"Right," said Zak Knight.

"I'm not!"

Zak Knight shrugged. "Whatever."

This guy, thought Norm, was **seriously** beginning to do his nut in. But whatever Norm did, he **knew** that he couldn't show it. The last thing he wanted was for Zak flipping Knight to feel even smugger than he was obviously feeling already. But why? wondered Norm. Why **was** he feeling so smug and pleased with himself?

"Sorry, Norm," said Mikey awkwardly. "But Zak **did** ask first."

"'S'okay, Mikey," said Norm.

"Not that it would've made any difference," said Zak Knight.

Norm pulled a face. "What's **that** supposed to mean?"

Zak Knight shrugged again. "It wouldn't have made any difference **who** asked first. I mean, there's no contest, is there?"

By now Norm knew better than to ask Zak Knight what he meant. But there was no need to ask anyway. There was no **way** Zak Knight was going to miss an opportunity to make Norm feel even **more** rubbish. And sure enough he didn't.

"Ninety-six-inch flat-screen HD TV?

A wide selection of completely inappropriate Xbox games?

Allowed to go to bed literally any time we want?"

Zak Knight paused for maximum effect.

"What's not to like?"

Nothing, thought Norm. Abso-flipping-lutely **nothing**. A ninety-six-inch TV? That was like...like...like... Norm couldn't actually think what it was like, but he was pretty sure he'd been to cinemas with smaller screens that **that**.

"We might even pull an all-nighter," said Zak Knight. "What do you reckon, Mikey?"

But Mikey said nothing. He looked even **more** uncomfortable than before.

"Mikey?" said Zak Knight.

"Yeah?" said Mikey.

"I said, we might even pull an all-nighter."

"What?" said Mikey.

"You know? Stay up all night?"

"Oh, right," said Mikey. "Dunno. Maybe."

That was it, thought Norm. Zak Knight had clearly wanted to make a point. And now he'd flipping well made it. Well, whatever his game was, enough was enough. Norm's humiliation was complete. If Zak flipping Knight wanted to have Mikey for a sleepover *that* badly, he could flipping well have him. It was time to leave.

"See ya, Norm," muttered Mikey, as Norm and John turned to go.

"See ya," said Norm.

"You can stay if you want," said Zak Knight.

Norm turned round. "What?"

Zak Knight grinned.
"I was talking to
the dog." ,

CHAPTER 15

Norm didn't notice much, walking home from Mikey's with John. Not that Norm **ever** noticed much walking home from Mikey's, or indeed much full stop. But as he trudged slowly through the precinct, Norm seemed to notice even **less** than normal. He **didn't** notice that the sun was starting to sink below the horizon, for instance. Or that his stomach was beginning to rumble because he never had got round to having breakfast that morning – and he'd hardly eaten anything for lunch.

So it wasn't exactly a **major** surprise when Norm **didn't** notice Zak Knight's sister, Alice, suddenly step out of the late-afternoon shadows and stand directly in front of him, blocking his path.

"Hi, Norman."

"AAAAAAAAAAARGH!" screamed Norm.

WOOF! went John.

"What's the matter?" laughed Alice. "You look like you've just seen a **ghost**!"

Funny she should say that, thought Norm. Or rather, *not* funny she should say that. Because a ghost was **precisely** what Norm had just thought he'd seen. Or a vampire, anyway. What with the stark contrast between her dark clothes and her pale face, it was as if Alice was in black-and-white and everything else was in colour.

"I didn't know you'd got a dog, by the way."

"I haven't," said Norm.

Alice pulled a face. "Really? Looks like you've got one to me."

"What?" said Norm. "No, I mean, it's my brothers' dog. Not mine."

"Oh, I see," said Alice. "What's his name?"

"Brian and Dave," said Norm. "I've got two."

Alice laughed. "I meant, what's the **dog's** name?"

"Oh, right," said Norm. "John."

"Hello, John," said Alice, bending down and ruffling John's fur.

WOOF! went John.

"Sorry," said Norm. "I was..."

"What?" said Alice. "In a world of your own?"

Norm shrugged. "Yeah, kind of."

"I know exactly how you feel," said Alice.

Norm doubted that very much. Alice couldn't possibly know **exactly** how he felt. Not unless **her** best friend had suddenly dumped **her** in favour of the single most annoying person in the entire history of the flipping planet. More annoying even than his two brothers and Chelsea all rolled into one – and **that** was flipping saying something!

"Really?" said Norm.

Alice nodded.
"Totally."

"Do you know
what's happened?"
said Norm.

"When?"

"Just now."

Alice shrugged. "No. What?"

Norm sighed. "Long story."

"Excellent!" said Alice.

"Uh?" said Norm.

"I love a good story," said Alice. "Which way are you going?"

Norm thought for a moment. Wasn't it pretty flipping **obvious** which way he was going? Straight ahead!

"Sorry," said Alice. "Stupid question."

Norm **almost** smiled. "It was a bit."

"Let's go," said Alice, setting off in the direction Norm had been heading in the first place.

Norm was relieved to discover that it wasn't too difficult to keep up with Alice. Alice seemed about as reluctant to break any land speed records as **he** did – though how much of that was due to the sheer weight of her massive clumpy boots was hard to tell.

"Come on, then," said Alice. "Once upon a time..."

Norm exhaled noisily. "Actually, it's a bit..."

"A bit what?"

"Awkward".

"Awkward?" said Alice.

Norm nodded.

"Let me guess," said Alice. "This is about my brother, isn't it? My *little* brother?"

Norm nodded again.

"I knew it," said Alice. "The thing is..."

What? thought Norm. What was the thing?

"The thing is..."

Gordon flipping Bennet! thought Norm. Was she going to tell him what the flipping thing was or was he going to have to guess?

"Zak's..."

What? thought Norm, getting more and more exasperated. Allergic to cheese?

Half-human, half-penguin?

A virtuoso on the trumpet?

"Got issues."

Uh? thought Norm. Issues? What, like magazines, or something? Because if **they** were the sort of issues Alice meant, Norm had plenty of **those**!

"He's actually quite shy."

Norm pulled a face. He must have misheard.

"I know what you're thinking, Norman."

"Do you?"

"Yeah, you're thinking, 'Zak Knight? Shy? Pull the other one!'"

Norm was confused. Pull the other *what*?

Alice laughed. "I don't *blame* you."

"What for?"

"For thinking that."

"Really?" said Norm, who was perfectly used to being blamed for stuff, but not *quite* so used to *not* being blamed for stuff. He just pretty much *assumed* everything was his fault these days.

"Course not," said Alice. "I know Zak can come across as dead cocky and confident and..."

"Showy-offy?" said Norm, not even sure whether that was a proper word or not.

Alice laughed again. "Yeah. Showy-offy."

Norm could sense a **but** coming. "Are you going to tell me he's not **really** like that, or something?"

"Well, yeah," said Alice. "Actually, I am."

They carried on walking for a few seconds. Norm was finding it very hard to believe that Zak Knight was anything other than a complete and utter doughnut. But Alice had helped him out of a tight spot earlier on. The least Norm could do **now** was listen to what she had to say.

"It's a security blanket thing."

Whoa, thought Norm. Zak Knight had a security blanket? Now *that* was the sort of information that could come in **very** useful. Post it on Facebook and **everybody** would know! That'd flipping show him!

"I don't mean he's *literally* got a security blanket, by the way," said Alice.

"Oh," said Norm. "I mean, course not. I knew that."

"I mean he's insecure and that he covers that up by being..."

"A prize doughnut?" said Norm.

"Well, yeah, basically," said Alice. "Does that make sense?"

Not really, thought Norm. Why should Zak flipping Knight get away with acting like an idiot just because he was 'shy'?

Norm just wasn't buying it. Where would it end? **Sorry I didn't do my homework, Miss. I'm shy?** Actually, thought Norm, that wasn't such a bad idea, thinking about it. He might try that next time.

"Sometimes he...overcompensates."

Overwhat? thought Norm.

"You know?" said Alice. "Goes too far the other way and ends up coming across as being overly confident?"

Uh? thought Norm. What did she keep coming out with all these big fancy words for? What did she want? A flipping medal or something?

A phone rang. Norm's phone. Norm fished it out of his pocket and answered.

"Hello?" said Norm. "Oh, hi, Mum."

Norm glanced at Alice. This wasn't cool. This wasn't cool at all.

"IKEA? What, *now*? But..."

Norm thought for a moment while he desperately tried to come up with a *but*...

"I still haven't tidied my room!"

Norm listened.

"Yeah, promise, Mum. 'Kay, Mum. Sorry, Mum. Bye, Mum."

Norm ended the call and pocketed his phone again.

"IKEA?" said Alice. "On a Saturday night?"

"*So* embarrassing," mumbled Norm.

Alice grinned. "Welcome to my world."

Norm looked at Alice. "Seriously? Your parents go to IKEA on a Saturday night as well?"

"Parent," said Alice.

"What?" said Norm.

"Parent – not **parents**," said Alice. "I've only got one."

Norm didn't know what to say. All of a sudden, sleepovers didn't seem quite so important. "Sorry, I didn't..."

Alice shrugged. "It's OK. Stuff happens."

Certainly does, thought Norm.

"Don't let me keep you," said Alice.

"What?" said Norm.

"If you need to tidy your room?"

"Oh, right. Yeah."

"You **really** don't want to go to IKEA, do you?"

"Who **does**?" said Norm.

Alice laughed. "I like you, Norman."

Norm instantly felt himself going bright red. It was

a good job it was quite gloomy. With any luck Alice wouldn't even notice.

"Not like **that**, obviously," said Alice.

Like **what** then? thought Norm. Like when you liked something on Facebook?

"You're much too young. How old are you?"

"Nearly thirteen," said Norm.

"There you go then," said Alice. "I'm nearly fourteen. And girls are much more mature than boys, anyway. So actually that's the equivalent of me being about **ten** years older than you."

Uh? thought Norm. **Girls** more mature than **boys**? What a load of skid-mark-encrusted pants **that** was!

"Can I ask you a question?" said Norm.

"I dunno," said Alice. "Can you?"

"Why did Zak call you **Dark** Alice?"

"Dark **alleys**?" said Alice. "As in 'I wouldn't like to meet her down a dark alley'?"

Norm looked puzzled. "I don't geddit."

"Don't worry about it," said Alice. "It's not even funny."

By now they'd reached not only the end of the conversation, but also the end of the street.

"See you, then," said Norm, heading off in one direction with John.

"You never did tell me the end of the story!" called Alice, heading off in the other direction.

"Some other time," yelled Norm.

CHAPTER 16

There was a note on the kitchen table when
Norm got in.
He picked it up
and read:

Help yourself
to anything in
the fridge
Love, Mum

Norm didn't need telling twice. When it came to
food, Norm didn't **usually** need telling **once** – let
alone **twice** – but by now
it was late afternoon, and
he'd **still** hardly eaten
anything all day. It wasn't
his fault though. How was
he supposed to know that
he'd slip on some dog sick

and hurt his wrist and not be able to go biking

and be made to get a
cauliflower instead

and then bump into
someone he wished he
hadn't bumped into

and be rejected by his best friend

and then have to tidy
his flipping room?

Mind you, thought Norm, it could've been worse. At least he hadn't had to go to IKEA.

Norm opened the fridge and stared, open-mouthed. There was abso-flipping-lutely **nothing** there! Apart from some eggs, and frankly Norm wouldn't have known what to do with a flipping egg if his life depended on it. Anyway, eggs came out of chickens' bottoms and were therefore basically evil.  Apart from the eggs though, the fridge was completely bare. Well, there were a few jars of stuff that looked like they'd be better off in the cupboard under the sink, along with the washing-up liquid and the bleach. There were a few vegetables too, but vegetables didn't count because vegetables weren't actually proper food as far as Norm was concerned. There was also a plastic container full of what looked suspiciously like leftover cauliflower cheese – but Norm would sooner have eaten the actual container than leftover cauliflower cheese. Apart from **that**, though, the fridge was completely empty.

Some people were **SO** flipping inconsiderate, thought Norm. What was he supposed to do now? Wait till his mum and dad got back and hope that they'd called at the supermarket on the way? How long was **that** going to be? Norm might literally have starved by then. It'd serve them flipping right if he had. They could've at least left some money for him to phone for a pizza or something!

Wait a minute, thought Norm. Pizza? Of course! That was it! Pizza! The one he'd discovered in his room! Genius. Why hadn't he thought of that before?

In a matter of seconds Norm had bounded up the stairs and dived under his bed. The pizza was still there, where he'd left it earlier. There was no need to reheat it. It would be just fine as it was. In fact, thought Norm, he didn't even have to eat it in his bedroom if he didn't want to. No one was around to boss him about or to tell him what he could or couldn't do. He could eat it anywhere he wanted. Whilst doing **whatever** he wanted to do!

What was that expression? wondered Norm. While the cat was away the mice would play? Well, while the **cats** were away, the **mouse** would play, anyway. Did mice like pizza? wondered Norm. Who flipping cared? **He** did.

It never even occurred to Norm to wonder how **long** the pizza had been under his bed **before** he'd discovered it. He never stopped to think exactly **how** it had come to be there – or **where** it had come from. And anyway, even if he **had**, it wouldn't have made the slightest bit of difference to Norm – or made the prospect of scoffing it any less mouthwatering. Pizza was pizza as far as Norm was concerned – the food of ancient gods, invented by the Romans along with straight roads, microwaves, the internet and zebras. But pizza was the big one. The one they'd be remembered for. The one that had **truly** changed the world. Well, it had changed **Norm's** world, anyway. From the moment he sank his teeth into his first ever slice of deep pan margherita, Norm knew that life would never, ever be the same again. There was no turning back.

There was **definitely** no turning back now as Norm grabbed the box and headed for the bathroom.

CHAPTER 17

It wasn't easy sitting on the toilet, checking Facebook **and** eating pizza at the same time – but Norm soon got the hang of it. And anyway, it wasn't like he had a choice. He **needed** to eat and he **needed** to check Facebook to see what – if anything – was going on. It wasn't **his** flipping fault that the only place he could do **both** was the bathroom.

PIZZA

What Norm needed to do **most** of all, though, was think for a while – take stock of the situation and preferably work out some kind of plan. What better place to do that, thought Norm, than sitting on the toilet? And what better **time** to do that than when everyone else was out?

The problem was, Norm couldn't sit down and come up with a plan to wreak horrible revenge on Zak Knight just like that. A plan, as far as Norm was concerned, was like a burp. It either popped into your head, or it didn't. Norm sighed. He never had been able to burp on demand like some people could. It was so unfair. Not only that, Norm still couldn't quite believe he had  the sort of parents whose idea of a good night out was going to IKEA. Not just **any** old night, either. **Saturday** night! That wasn't merely uncool – that was positively Antarctic. What if someone saw them and word got out? Norm could quite literally die of embarrassment. In fact, thought Norm, he really should have a word with his mum and dad.

If they insisted on going, they could at least wear a flipping disguise!

Norm felt a sudden stab of guilt as he remembered what Alice had told him earlier. About only having one parent. She never had got round to saying which one though. Or what had happened to the other. She'd just kind of laughed it off. Almost as if she hadn't wanted to talk about it. Well, Norm knew exactly how *that* felt. He quite often didn't want to talk about stuff – and the *more* someone asked him about it, the *more* he didn't want to talk about it. So if Alice didn't want to talk about why she only had one parent, that was fine by Norm. No probs whatso-flipping-ever.

Norm took another bite of pizza. Admittedly, it wasn't the **best** he'd ever tasted, but it was by no means the **worst**, either. OK, so the base was a bit chewy, and he could definitely have done without the sweet corn – but all in all it wasn't **too** bad. Then again, Norm was so hungry it could've tasted like the back  end of a horse for all he cared. He still would have eaten it.

And then it happened. What Norm had been half expecting, but mainly half dreading. A post on Facebook. Not just any old post on Facebook, either. A post on Facebook from Zak flipping Knight because he'd gone and tagged himself with Mikey. Oh well, thought Norm. It had only been a matter of time. And now that time had come. He might as well look and get it over with.

Zak Knight
"Jus chillin wiv my main man Mikey. Let the mayhem begin lol!"

Norm didn't know where to start. **Main man** Mikey? Was he serious? If Mikey was **anyone's** main man, he was **Norm's** main man – not Zak flipping Knight's! As for **mayhem**? What was **that** supposed to even **mean**? Mayhem? What? Staying up late and playing on the Xbox?

"What a doughnut," muttered Norm.

"Who is?" said Chelsea, from the doorway.

"AAAAAAAAAAARGH!" screamed Norm for at least the third time that day. Not that he was keeping count. And not that it would have made any difference if he **had** been keeping count. He still would have screamed.

Chelsea laughed. "What do you expect?"

"Uh?" said Norm.

"Well, if you **will** keep leaving doors open, **Norman**."

What? thought Norm. This girl was unbe-flipping-lievable! And not in a good way, either. "There's no one else in! There was no **need** to close the flipping door!"

"Not the **bathroom** door," said Chelsea. "The **front** door!"

"What?" said Norm.

"The **front** door," said Chelsea. "It was open. **Again**!"

"Oh, right," said Norm. "But you still can't just..."

"What?" said Chelsea innocently. "I noticed the car wasn't there."

"Yeah? So?" said Norm.

"So I put two and two together!"

"Yeah, you did, didn't you?" said Norm. "And got flipping five!"

$$2+2=5$$

"I was just being a good neighbour!" said Chelsea. "There might have been a break-in."

"Yeah, well, there wasn't, was there?" snapped Norm. "And anyway, what if there **had** been? What would you have done?"

Chelsea shrugged. "Not sure."

Brilliant, thought Norm. He knew there was no point arguing though. Nothing was going to change Chelsea's mind. **She** was right. **He** was wrong. End of. Still, thought Norm, it could've been a lot worse. After all, he was only sitting on **top** of the toilet. It wasn't like he was actually **on** the toilet. Now **that** really **would** have been embarrassing. And frankly, things were embarrassing enough as they were.

Chelsea pulled a face. "Are you eating pizza?"

Norm sighed. Course he was eating pizza! What it did it flipping *look* like he was doing? "Yeah. Want some?"

"Are you serious?" said Chelsea. "It looks

absolutely minging!"

"Suit yourself," said Norm.

Chelsea laughed.

"What?"

"Pizza in the bathroom," said Chelsea. "You certainly know how to win a girl's heart, **_Norman_**."

Norm was mortified. "What?"

"And they say romance is dead."

Norm could feel himself going bright red. That wasn't what he'd meant. He'd just figured that if he offered Chelsea some pizza then perhaps she'd go. But she just wouldn't take a flipping hint.

"So who's a doughnut then?" said Chelsea, sitting down on the side of the bath, clearly not intending to go anywhere for a good while yet.

"Uh?"

"Who's a doughnut?"

"Oh, right," said Norm. "Zak Knight."

"Who?" said Chelsea.

"Zak Knight," said Norm. "Hal's brother."

"Oh, right," said Chelsea dreamily. "He's lovely!"

What? thought Norm. Zak Knight was many things. But *lovely* wasn't one of them. Was Chelsea out of her mind?

"Hal, I mean." said Chelsea. "Obviously."

"Er, yeah," said Norm. "Obviously."

"I don't know Zak."

"You wouldn't flipping **want** to," muttered Norm.

"Why? What's wrong with him?" said Chelsea.

Norm sighed. "What's **right** with him, more like."

"Hmm," said Chelsea. "Like that, is it?"

But Norm wasn't listening. He'd had a thought. "Can I ask you a question?"

Chelsea grinned. "I don't know, **Norman**. Can you?"

"What's it like to…"

"What?" said Chelsea.

"You know."

"No, I don't, actually," said Chelsea. "Gimme a clue."

Norm hesitated. "Only have one…"

"One **what**?" said Chelsea. "One head? You need to be more specific than that, **Norman**!"

"Parent," said Norm. "What's it like to only have one parent?"

Chelsea shrugged. "I've no idea."

"But…"

"But what?" said Chelsea. "I've got two parents. They just happen to live in different houses, that's all."

"Oh, yeah," mumbled Norm. "Forgot."

It was true. Norm **had** temporarily forgotten that Chelsea only lived next door with her dad at weekends – mercifully spending the other five days with her mum. If only **he** could come to some sort of similar arrangement regarding living with his brothers. Life would be **SO** much more tolerable.

"Why do you ask, anyway?" said Chelsea.

Norm wasn't actually sure why he'd asked. He'd somehow imagined there might be a connection between having one parent and being a complete doughnut. But thinking about it now, thought Norm, thinking about it, that did seem pretty far-fetched.

"Zak Knight's only got one parent."

Chelsea shrugged again. "So? It's no big deal. Loads of kids only have one parent."

"Yeah, I know, but..."

"But what?"

Norm sighed. "Oh, I dunno."

"Yeah, well, when you do, let me know, **_Norman_**."

Norm took a bite of pizza.

"Mmmm, yum," said Chelsea. "I think I might have changed my mind."

"Really?" said Norm.

"Nah, not really," said Chelsea. "So why's he a doughnut anyway?"

"What?" said Norm.

"Zak Knight. Why's he a doughnut?"

"He just is."

Chelsea studied Norm for a moment as if he was some kind of inferior life form. "He just *is*?"

Norm nodded.

"Hmm, well, there's nothing like a well-thought-out argument," said Chelsea. "And that's **nothing** like a well-thought-out argument."

But Norm wasn't listening again. He'd just noticed another post from Zak Knight on Facebook.

Zak Knight

"Revenge of the sheep.
Gonna be totally awesome!"

Norm glanced up to see Chelsea looking at him expectantly. "Do you mind?"

"Do I mind what, **_Norman_**?"

Norm didn't know where to start. So he didn't bother.

"Can you **_go_**, please?"

"All right, all right," said Chelsea, turning and heading for the stairs.

"AND SHUT THE FLIPPING FRONT DOOR BEHIND YOU!!!" yelled Norm.

CHAPTER 18

Norm was coming out of the bathroom carrying his iPad and the pizza box when he came face to face with his mum.

"Hello, love."

"What?"

Norm's mum smiled. "I just said hello, that's all, love."

"Oh, right," said Norm. "Hi, Mum."

Norm was, it has to be said, slightly distracted. Actually, Norm was slightly more than **slightly** distracted. Norm was **very** distracted – and had been ever since he'd read Zak Knight's latest post on Facebook. Revenge of the sheep? What was **that** supposed to be when it was at home? One of the so-called 'completely inappropriate' Xbox games he was going on about earlier? If so, thought Norm, it didn't sound completely inappropriate, it sounded completely rubbish – and not in the least bit awesome, never mind **totally** awesome.

"What have you been doing in there?" asked Norm's mum suspiciously.

Norm pulled a face. "What do you mean, Mum?"

"Well, I couldn't help noticing you've got your iPad with you."

"Oh right," said Norm. "I've been checking Facebook."

"In the bathroom?" said Norm's mum.

"It's the only place I can get a decent signal, Mum!"

"I was only asking," said Norm's mum. "And the pizza box?"

Norm shrugged. "I was hungry."

Norm's mum laughed. "Ask a silly question!"

"What?"

"Wait a minute," said Norm's mum, examining the pizza box more closely. "Where did you find **that**?"

Norm thought for a moment. Should he say or not? "Under the bed."

"**Your** bed?"

Was his mum *serious*? thought Norm. Of **course** he'd found the pizza under his own bed! Where did she **think** he'd found it? Under someone **else's** bed? That would be disgusting!

"How did it get there, love?"

"Erm…" said Norm. "Not sure."

"Not sure?"

"Can't remember, Mum," said Norm. "Why?"

"Why?" said Norm's mum.

Norm nodded.

"Because I'm **pretty** sure that's the same pizza I threw away about a week ago!"

A week ago? thought Norm. No wonder the base was a bit chewy!

"Let me see, love."

Norm handed his mum the pizza box.

"Yes, that's the one," said Norm's mum, reading the label. "Wikipizza."

Something was troubling Norm. How could **anyone** in their right mind **ever** get rid of a pizza? It was completely beyond his comprehension. It just didn't compute.

"But..."

"But what?" said Norm's mum.

"Why?"

"Why what, love?"

"Why did you throw it away?"

"It had gone off."

Gone off? thought Norm. Where to?

"It was past its sell-by date."

"Oh," said Norm.

"What did it taste like?"

Norm shrugged. "All right."

"Well, I think I'd better throw it away," said Norm's mum. "Again!"

"But..."

"But what, love?"

"There's still one slice left," said Norm.

"Hang on," said Norm's mum, ignoring Norm's pleas.

"What is it?" said Norm.

"There are teeth marks in the box!"

Norm hadn't noticed before, but his mum was right. There **were** teeth marks in the pizza box. Norm knew he'd been hungry – but he didn't think he'd been *that* hungry!

"Do you know what I think has happened?"

"What, Mum?"

"I think John might have sniffed it out in the bin after I threw it away!"

"What?" said Norm.

Norm's mum nodded. "Then hidden it under your bed."

Norm hated to admit it, but it did sound vaguely feasible. As well as completely gross.

"I could be wrong," said Norm's mum.

Flipping hope so, thought Norm.

"I mean, it could've been one of your brothers."

"Why don't you ask them, Mum?"

"I will when they get back."

Get back? thought Norm. Were Brian and Dave not at home, then? Come to think of it, the house **was** pretty quiet.

"Get back from where, Mum?" said Norm.

"Oh, did we not tell you, love? They've been invited for sleepovers."

What? thought Norm. His little brothers had been invited for sleepovers? No flipping way! This was obviously some kind of sick joke. In fact, he was probably being filmed by hidden cameras as part of some stupid reality TV programme right now, and no one had bothered to tell him. Well, **obviously** no one had bothered to tell him. That was the whole point of the programme, presumably. And anyway, thought Norm, since when had his stupid little brothers had any friends?

"Isn't that great?" Norm's mum smiled.

No, thought Norm. It wasn't great. It wasn't great at all. In fact it was the **opposite** of great. It was like… it was like…it was like…**un**great, that's what it was like. Like a slap in the face with a dirty great wet fish. Yeah, thought Norm. That was **exactly** what it was like!

"Norman?"

"What?"

"I said, isn't that great?" said Norm's mum. "It means you and Mikey can have the place to yourselves!"

"Uh?"

"When Mikey comes **here** for a sleepover! Where is he, by the way?"

"Oh, right," said Norm. "About that, Mum."

"What about it, love?"

"It's not happening."

Norm's mum looked surprised. "Oh. Why not?"

Hmm, thought Norm. What should he say? That he'd been dropped like a hot potato by his so-called **best** friend in favour of some kid who thinks he's flipping **it**? Yeah, right.

"Well, love?"

"He's ill."

"Mikey?"

Norm nodded.

"What's the matter with him?"

"Been sick."

"Aw, poor Mikey," said Norm's mum.

Yeah, thought Norm bitterly. Poor Mikey.

"Oh well," said Norm's mum. "How's that room of yours looking?"

Oops, thought Norm. Not only was his room looking **exactly** the same as it had done earlier, he'd completely forgotten that he was even supposed to be tidying it. It was hardly surprising, what with everything else that had been going on. But his mum wasn't to know that, was she?

Norm's mum smiled. "You haven't done it, have you?"

"Erm…" began Norm.

"It's OK, love."

Norm pulled a face. Had he heard right? "What, Mum?"

"It doesn't matter."

"What doesn't?"

"Tidying your room."

Norm was getting very confused. Why should something that had mattered all day long suddenly *not* matter? "But…"

yelled Norm's dad from the foot of the stairs.

196

"Yeah?" yelled Norm.

"Get down here!"

Gordon flipping Bennet, thought Norm. What now?

CHAPTER 19

"In your own time," said Norm's dad from the hall, as Norm sauntered down the stairs with all the urgency of a chilled-out snail.
"Preferably today."

Norm hated it when his dad was sarcastic. Or when **anybody** was sarcastic, for that matter. Apart from himself, of course. That was fine.

"Give me a hand with this, will you?" said Norm's dad.

"With what?"

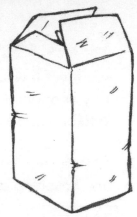

"This," said Norm's dad, indicating a large cardboard box – although still not large enough for Norm to have noticed.

"But..."

"But nothing, Norman. Just give me a hand."

Norm sighed. Seemingly just a *bit* too loudly.

"Of course, if it's too much trouble I can always do it myself," said Norm's dad, the vein on the side of his head starting to throb.

Norm thought briefly about mentioning his bad wrist, but given that he could no longer remember which wrist it was that he'd actually hurt, decided it was probably best not to.

"What is it, Dad?"

"It's a surprise, Norman."

Well, obviously it was a flipping *surprise*, thought Norm. *He* didn't know what was in the box. So whatever it was was **bound** to be a surprise one way or another, wasn't it? The question was, what **kind** of surprise was it?

"Come on," said Norm's dad, crouching down and grabbing one end.

Norm followed suit and grabbed the other end of the box.

"After three... Three!" said Norm's dad, standing up and lifting in one movement.

Gordon flipping Bennet, thought Norm, struggling to do the same. Whatever kind of surprise it was, it was a flipping heavy one.

"Up the stairs," said Norm's dad.

"What?" said Norm, as if his dad had just suggested he painted the entire house with a worn-out toothbrush.

"You heard."

Norm and his dad started climbing the stairs – Norm at the front, his dad at the back taking most of the weight. Not nearly **enough** of the weight as far as Norm was concerned, but as they were forever saying on the telly, every little helped.

"Where to now, Dad?" panted Norm when they reached the landing.

"Your room," said Norm's dad.

"*My* room?" said Norm.

Norm could feel himself beginning to get just a **little** bit excited. He knew he shouldn't. But surely **something** good was due to happen today. What could it be?

"What do you think, love? About here?" said Norm's mum as Norm appeared in his room.

Norm did his best to shrug, but it wasn't easy while he was still struggling to carry the box. "Dunno, Mum. What is it?"

"Oh, didn't Dad tell you?"

"I didn't want to spoil the surprise," grinned Norm's dad.

This had better be flipping worth it, thought Norm.

"Shall I tell him, or will you?" said Norm's mum.

"Don't know," said Norm's dad. "What do you think?"

"You tell him," said Norm's mum.

"No, *you* tell him," said Norm's dad.

"Dad?"

"Yes, Norman?"

"Can we put the box down now, please?"

"Oh, yes. Sorry," said Norm's dad.

Norm and his dad lowered the box to the floor.

"It's a chest of drawers, love!"

"What?"

"It's a chest of drawers!" repeated Norm's mum. "So you can put your things away properly! *That's* why I said it didn't matter that you hadn't tidied your room!"

Uh? thought Norm. So *that's* why his mum and dad had gone to IKEA. To get a chest of flipping drawers! He knew that he was expected to say something. But what *could* he say after all that build up and suspense? It was like raiding the biscuit tin and discovering that there was only *one* biscuit left – and that it was a flipping rich tea!

"Look," said Norm's dad. "He's speechless."

Norm's mum nodded. "I told you he'd be happy, didn't I?"

Happy? thought Norm. Oh, he was **happy** all right. Happy that any minute now he'd wake up and discover that this had all been one big nightmare. It was the only possible explanation for a day that had started off badly and had gone steadily downhill ever since. The only consolation was that things literally couldn't get any worse.

"Come on, then," said Norm's dad, opening the box. "Let's get cracking."

"What?" mumbled Norm.

Norm's dad laughed. "Well, you don't expect me to put this thing together myself, do you?"

Actually, thought Norm, that was **precisely** what he expected his dad to do. Why should **he** have to help? He hadn't **asked** them to go and get a flipping chest of drawers, had he? He was nearly thirteen – not nearly flipping thirty!

"Well?" said Norm's dad.

Norm sighed, trying desperately not to think of the things he **could** have been doing. All the things he **should** have been doing. All the things that Mikey and Zak flipping Knight probably **were** doing! He should have known not to think things literally couldn't get any **worse**. They just literally **had**!

"Unless you've got something better to do," said Norm's dad.

"Actually, Dad..." began Norm.

"What?" said Norm's dad, the vein on the side of his head instantly beginning to throb again. "No, don't tell me. You absolutely **have** to check Facebook right this second?"

Norm shook his head.

"What then?"

"I don't feel very well."

"What's the matter, love?" said Norm's mum gently.

"Feel sick," said Norm.

"Really?"

Norm nodded.

"Come on," said Norm's mum, taking Norm gently by the arm and ushering him towards his bed.

"Thanks, Mum," said Norm feebly, lying down.

"How convenient," said Norm's dad.

"What do you mean?" said Norm's mum.

"Feeling sick the second he thinks he might actually have to, you know, *do* something?"

"Alan!" said Norm's mum. "How could you be so cynical?"

"What?" said Norm's dad. "You don't think he's putting it on, then?"

"No, I do **not**!" said Norm's mum sharply. "Look at him. He's gone all white!"

"Sick my backside," muttered Norm's dad.

"I **am** feeling sick, Dad," said Norm. "Honest."

"Poor baby," said Norm's mum, feeling Norm's forehead with her hand. "You must have got the same thing Mikey's got."

"Ha!" said Norm's dad, clearly neither convinced nor impressed.

"I need a bucket," said Norm suddenly.

"What do you say?" said Norm's dad.

"BLEURGH!!!" said Norm, projectile-vomiting across the room and hitting his dad's slippers with unerring accuracy.

"Oh for goodness' **sake**, that's disgusting!" said Norm's dad. "Sweet corn?"

"There, there, don't listen to him, love," said Norm's mum soothingly. "Never liked those slippers anyway."

CHAPTER 20

Norm opened his eyes. Which was weird, thought Norm, because he couldn't actually remember *closing* them in the first place. He'd obviously fallen asleep for a few minutes.

Slowly but surely it all started coming back to him. Well, bits of it anyway. He'd been sick. On his dad. There'd been sweet corn. That much was certain.

Of course! thought Norm. The pizza! The *pizza* had obviously made him sick! Hardly surprising either. His mum had thrown it out a *week* ago. And it was already past its sell-by date then! Not that Norm had known that when he'd eaten it, of course.

And it probably wouldn't have stopped him eating it anyway. But it looked like his mum might well have been right. John really must have found the pizza in the bin and then hidden it under Norm's bed afterwards. And it was the **pizza** that had made **John** sick too. That's why there'd been bits of sweet corn in the sick that Norm had slipped on. **That's** why there'd been bits of sweetcorn in Norm's bed. John had been eating manky pizza in **his** flipping bed! And **that** was why Norm had woken up to find corn in his ear! It was the **only** possible explanation. And frankly, thought Norm, it was almost too gross to think about.

Norm rolled over and very nearly fell out of bed. Not because he'd rolled too close to the edge, but because he could hardly believe his eyes. A chest of drawers? Who put **that** there? What on earth was going on? He **had** woken up in the right house, hadn't he?

Norm looked around. Sure enough, there were the usual mountain biking posters on the walls, not to mention a distinct whiff of sick. Nope, thought

Norm. He was definitely in the right house, all right. Worse flipping luck.

"Morning, love," said Norm's mum, breezing into the room and opening not only the curtains but the window as well.

What? thought Norm. **Morning**? He'd obviously been asleep longer than he'd thought!

"How are you feeling?" said Norm's mum, sitting down on the bed and feeling Norm's forehead with the back of her hand.

"Better, thanks, Mum," mumbled Norm.

"That's good, love. You really were quite poorly, weren't you?"

Norm nodded.

"So what do you think, then?"

"To what?" said Norm.

"The chest of drawers?"

"Oh, right," said Norm.

"Dad spent *ages* assembling it last night," said Norm's mum. "You were sleeping like a baby! They're great, aren't they?"

Uh? thought Norm. What was his mum on about? Babies weren't great. Babies were rubbish. All they ever did was eat, sleep, poo and cry. Anybody could do *that*.

"You can paint them if you want," said Norm's mum.

Norm was getting confused. "What? Babies?"

"The chest of drawers," said Norm's mum.

"Oh, right," said Norm.

"Are you **sure** you're feeling OK, love?"

"I'm fine," said Norm. "I'm just a bit..."

"A bit what?"

It was a good question, thought Norm. A bit what? Groggy? Yes, that's what he was. A bit groggy. A little fuzzy round the edges. Like there was something he couldn't quite remember. But what? thought Norm. What *was* it that he couldn't quite remember?

"I wonder if Mikey's feeling any better," said Norm's mum.

It suddenly hit Norm like a tonne of bricks. **That** was it. **That** was what he couldn't quite remember. Or, more accurately, what he didn't **want** to remember. That **Mikey** had been invited to a sleepover at Zak flipping Knight's and he hadn't. That **Mikey** had no doubt been up all night playing Call of Grand Theft flipping Doom Raiders or  whatever on a TV the size of a football pitch at Zak flipping Knight's and he hadn't. More importantly, that **Mikey** had somehow managed to make an impression on Zak flipping Knight all those years ago – and **he** hadn't. But why? That's what **Norm** wanted to know. Why?

"What is it, love?"

Norm sighed. "Nothing, Mum."

"Sure?"

Norm nodded. "Sure, Mum."

214

WOOF! went John, exploding into the room without warning, launching himself at Norm and slobbering all over his face.

"GERRIMOFF ME!" yelled Norm.

"He's just being friendly, Norman!" said Brian, appearing in the doorway.

"Yeah, Norman," said Dave, appearing next to Brian. "He's just being friendly!"

"Actually, that **is** pretty disgusting," said Norm's mum, pulling John off Norm. "We don't want him catching anything else now, do we?"

"Who? John?" Dave laughed.

"Ha, ha, very funny," said Norm.

"Morning, boys!" said Norm's mum. "How were your sleepovers?"

"Great, thanks, Mum!" said Brian.

"Yeah, great, Mum!" said Dave.

"Excellent! Pleased to hear it!" said Norm's mum.

Yeah, **brilliant**, thought Norm. As if he didn't feel bad enough already about missing out. That was the icing on the flipping cake, that was. That his stupid little brothers had had a great time whilst he'd been busy throwing up flipping pizza! That was **just** what he needed to hear.

"Nice chest of drawers by the way," said Brian.

"Yeah, cool," said Dave.

"You're not **serious** are you, Dave?" said Norm.

"Course I'm serious," said Dave.

"You need to get out more," said Norm.

"Is there a problem?" said Norm's dad, appearing in the doorway behind Brian and Dave.

"Norman doesn't like the chest of drawers, Dad," said Brian.

"Oh, really?" said Norm's dad, the vein on the side of his head immediately beginning to throb.

"I didn't say that, Dad," said Norm.

"He kind of did, Dad," said Brian.

"Shut up, Brian, you flipping freak!"

"Language!" said Dave.

This was seriously starting to do Norm's nut in. Why couldn't everyone just leave him alone?

"Ah, so **this** is where everyone is," said Grandpa, **also** appearing in the doorway.

"Yeah! Grandpa!" sang Brian and Dave.

Gordon flipping Bennet, thought Norm. This was getting ridiculous. In fact, never mind **getting** ridiculous. It already **was** ridiculous!

"What's up, Norman?" said Grandpa. "You not feeling well, or something?"

"I'm all right," mumbled Norm.

"Hmmm," said Grandpa. "Looks like you could do with some fresh air to me. Get a bit of colour in those cheeks. Fancy a walk?"

Norm thought for a moment. For once in his life, he actually did.

CHAPTER 21

It was another beautiful morning. Even so, Norm still couldn't quite believe that he'd actually agreed to go for a walk **without** being physically removed from the house, and without **any** kind of financial incentive. But he had.

And he was glad that he had, too. Even if he **did** have a sneaking suspicion that Grandpa hadn't suggested it purely for the benefit of his health.

"Been feeling a bit rough then, have you, Norman?"

"You could say that, Grandpa," said Norm.

"I just did," said Grandpa.

Norm and Grandpa glanced at each other. Grandpa's eyes crinkled ever so slightly in the corners.

"Sick, were you?"

Norm nodded. "Pizza."

"Pizza, eh?" said Grandpa. "What a terrible waste."

Norm laughed. Yes, a walk with Grandpa was clearly **exactly** what he'd needed. Not only to help make him actually **feel** better, but to cheer him up a bit too.

"Any idea where we're going?" said Grandpa.

Norm pulled a face. He'd kind of hoped that Grandpa would know where they were going, because he hadn't been paying any attention.

"Are we lost, Grandpa?"

Grandpa's eyes crinkled slightly in the corners again. "No, we're not lost. I know where we're going. I just wondered if **you** did?"

"Erm," said Norm, looking around. "The allotments?"

"Correct," said Grandpa. "Any idea **why** we're going?"

Norm sighed. So **that** was why Grandpa had suggested going for a walk. He obviously needed help with something. Why did there **always** have to be a flipping catch? Just for once it would be nice if there wasn't.

"No idea?" said Grandpa.

But before Norm could reply, there was a beep from his phone. He'd got a text. Would it be from Mikey? Norm wasn't **expecting** to hear from him. Not after last night. He looked. It **was** from Mikey. Norm opened the text and read to himself...

It was nothing to do with me.

Uh? thought Norm. **What** was nothing to do with Mikey? What was he on about?

"What is it?" said Grandpa.

"What?" said Norm distractedly.

"I said what is it?"

"A text," said Norm.

Grandpa sighed. "I do actually know what texts **are**, you know. I meant, who is it **from**?"

"Oh, right," said Norm. "Mikey."

"Mikey, eh?" said Grandpa.

Norm nodded.

"How is he?"

But before Norm could reply, there was **another** beep from his phone.

"Don't mind me," said Grandpa.

Norm opened the text and read.

Tried to stop him but couldn't.

Tried to stop who? thought Norm. And perhaps
more importantly, from doing what? What was
going on? Or rather, what had already
gone on? Norm was getting a bad
feeling. And not a feeling like he
was about to be sick again. Like
he was about to find something
out. Something he'd rather not
find out. Something bad. But
just how bad could things get?
What was the worst that could
actually happen?

"Earth to Norman?"

"What?" said Norm.

"I said, we're here," said Grandpa.

"Oh, right," said Norm.

"You were miles away."

Yeah, thought Norm. Not as many miles away as he'd like to be. But it was a start.

Grandpa opened the gate to the allotments, before ushering Norm through and following him up the path.

"Notice anything, Norman?"

Norm hated it when someone asked him that. Mainly because the chances were he hadn't noticed anything. How did he even know what he was supposed to be noticing? It was so annoying.

"No?" said Grandpa. "Shall I give you a clue?"

Norm sighed. "Can you just tell me, please, Grandpa?"

Grandpa shrugged. "Okey-dokey. Look at my shed."

Gordon flipping Bennet! thought Norm as he did as he was told and looked at Grandpa's shed. Three words had been painted on one side in huge uneven letters:

"Now do you notice anything?" said Grandpa.

"Yeah," said Norm. "The spelling's terrible."

Norm turned to find Grandpa looking at him, one cloud-like eyebrow raised in exasperation.

"What?" protested Norm. "Well, I didn't do it, Grandpa! I've been ill in bed, haven't I?"

"I know you didn't do it, Norman."

"Pardon?" said Norm.

"I know you didn't do it," repeated Grandpa. "You might be daft, but you're not that daft!"

Norm thought for a moment. Was that supposed to be a compliment or not? Either way, at least

Grandpa knew that he hadn't done it. As if he would have actually painted his own name on Grandpa's shed. But clearly whoever **had** painted Norm's name on the shed wanted it to appear that Norm had done it himself, and get Norm into trouble. What a doughnut, thought Norm. But at least that would explain the texts from Mikey. Not that Norm thought for a single second that Mikey had done it. But this was obviously the 'mayhem' that Zak flipping Knight had been threatening to cause – vandalising Grandpa's shed! But why? Why would he want to do that? What had Norm ever done to him? That's what Norm still couldn't work out.

"Come here a minute," said Grandpa, disappearing round the other side of the shed.

Norm followed.

"What do you make of that?"

"What?" said Norm.

"That," said Grandpa.

Norm looked. Just the one word had been painted on this side of the shed.

"Doesn't make any sense," said Grandpa.

Norm thought for a moment. "Revenge of the sheep."

"Pardon?" said Grandpa, giving Norm a strange look.

"Er, nothing, Grandpa," said Norm. "Just something I saw on Facebook." Norm looked at Grandpa for a moment.

"I **know** what Facebook is," said Grandpa, his eyes crinkling slightly in the corners.

CHAPTER 22

Norm was still deep in thought as he trudged slowly back up his drive. It was all still a bit of a mystery. Actually, thought Norm, it was all still a **lot** of a mystery. OK, so Zak Knight didn't like him. So what? Who cared? Boo flipping hoo. But what had that got to do with flipping **sheep**?

"Baaa," said Norm, opening the front door and stepping into the hall.

"What was that, love?" said Norm's mum, appearing from the kitchen.

"Er, nothing, Mum," said Norm, closing the door behind him again. "I was just, er…"

Norm's mum looked at Norm for a moment.

"What, Mum?"

"Are you feeling OK?"

"I'm fine, Mum."

"Sure?"

"Sure, Mum."

"Sure you're sure?"

Norm sighed. "Sure I'm sure, Mum."

"Mikey's here, by the way."

Norm's face dropped. "What?"

"Mikey's here," repeated Norm's mum.

"Where?" said Norm anxiously.

"In the front room. Watching telly."

"Right."

"Has something happened?" said Norm's mum.

"No," said Norm, a bit too quickly. "What makes you think that?"

"It's just that you seem a bit surprised."

"Do I?" said Norm.

Norm's mum nodded.

"I'm not surprised," said Norm. "I'm not surprised at all."

"Good," said Norm's mum. "In that case you'd better go in and see him then, hadn't you?"

"Yeah, of course," said Norm, still showing no sign of going anywhere for the time being.

"Well, go on then, love."

"What?" said Norm.

"Off you go!"

"Oh, right."

Norm headed for the front room, suddenly unsure what to think, or say, or do. The only consolation as far as Norm was concerned was that knowing Mikey as well as he did, Mikey would be feeling **exactly** the same. If not **worse**.

"Hi, Norm," said Mikey, without taking his eyes off the TV.

"Hi," mumbled Norm.

There was an awkward pause.

"Have a seat," said Mikey eventually.

Uh? thought Norm. What was Mikey on about? Whose flipping house *was* this?

"It was a joke," said Mikey, nervously glancing up at Norm.

"Oh, right," said Norm, sitting down.

"I'm sorry," said Mikey.

"Should flipping think so too," said Norm. "It was a rubbish joke."

"No, I meant…"

"Oh, I see," said Norm.

There was another pause, only slightly longer this time.

"I know you didn't do it, Mikey."

"I know," said Mikey.

Norm pulled a face. "You know that I know you didn't do it?"

Mikey nodded again. "I still feel like it's all my fault though."

"But…" began Norm.

"No, really, I do, Norm. I should never have said yes."

"To what?" said Norm.

"The sleepover."

"Right."

"I should have made up an excuse, but..."

"What?" said Norm.

Mikey sighed. "I dunno. I just felt sorry for him."

Norm suddenly remembered about Zak Knight only having one parent. "You mean...?"

"Yeah," said Mikey. "I can't imagine what that must be like."

Norm suddenly felt really bad. Perhaps he **had** been a bit harsh about Zak Knight and what a doughnut he was. And perhaps it **was** true what Alice had said about Zak actually being really shy and stuff. But that still didn't explain **why**

he appeared to have singled **Norm** out for special treatment. And it **definitely** didn't excuse what he'd done to Grandpa's shed.

By now, Norm had a pretty good idea that Zak Knight had posted the comments on Facebook knowing full **well** that Norm would see them. That was obviously all part of his cunning plan. To wind Norm up as much as possible. And the really annoying part was that he'd flipping well gone and done it! Not that Norm wanted Zak to **know** that of course.

"I only ended up hanging out with him because you couldn't come out biking, Norm! Honest!"

"Yeah, I know that, Mikey. It's OK."

"Really?" said Mikey.

"Course," said Norm.

Mikey looked visibly relieved. As if a great weight had been lifted off his shoulders. "I feel used."

Uh? thought Norm. Used? What was Mikey on about now?

"I think he chose me *deliberately*."

"Yeah?" said Norm.

Mikey nodded. "He knew that you and me used to be friends."

Norm pulled a face. "**Used** to be?"

"When he lived here before," said Mikey.

"Oh, right," said Norm. "I see what you mean."

"I think he's got some kind of grudge."

"Grudge?" said Norm. "Against who?"

"You!" said Mikey.

"Me?" said Norm.

Mikey nodded.

"But..."

"What?" said Mikey.

"He said he didn't remember me."

"Ah, well, you see, that's the thing, Norm."

What was the thing? wondered Norm.

"I think he was only **pretending** not to remember you," said Mikey.

"Uh?" said Norm. "Seriously? Why would he do that?"

Mikey shrugged. "I dunno. To make you feel rubbish, I suppose."

Norm nodded. He hated to admit it, but in a funny kind of way he was actually beginning to admire Zak Knight. Didn't mean he had to *like* him. But there was something quite devious and calculating about him. Whatever it was he'd been trying to do, he'd obviously thought about it pretty thoroughly and hadn't simply gone charging in, like a bull in a greenhouse – or whatever the expression was.

"You know what else I think?" said Mikey.

"What?" said Norm.

"I don't think he really wanted to be **my** friend at all."

"Seriously?" said Norm.

"Seriously," said Mikey.

Norm thought about this for a moment. And the more he thought about it, the more angry he started to get. Messing with **him** was one thing.

GRRRRR

Messing with **Mikey** was another thing altogether. Shy or not, Zak flipping Knight needed to be taught a lesson.

"Fancy going biking, Mikey?" said Norm.

"Biking?" said Mikey. "But..."

"What?"

"What about your wrist, Norm?"

Norm shrugged. "What about it?"

"It's better, then?"

Norm nodded. "Much."

There was another pause.

"I'm sorry, Norm."

Norm looked confused. "What? You're sorry my wrist's better?"

"No," said Mikey.

Norm looked even **more** confused. "You're **not** sorry my wrist's better?"

Mikey sighed. "I'm sorry about last night."

"Oh, right," said Norm, finally twigging. "Don't worry about it, Mikey."

"What?" said Mikey.

"I said don't worry about it."

"But..."

"Mikey?"

"Yeah?" said Mikey.

"Shut it, you doughnut!" laughed Norm, heading for the door. "Are you coming, or what?"

CHAPTER 23

Even as Norm and Mikey cycled down the road, Norm had no idea what he'd say or do when he ran into Zak Knight. Or rather, Norm had no idea what he'd say or do *if* he ran into Zak Knight. There was no guarantee that it was actually going to happen. He didn't know where he lived. All Norm knew was that it was **unlikely** to happen if he and Mikey stayed in and didn't do something soon.

"So what was it like then, Mikey?"

"What was **what** like?" said Mikey, knowing full well what Norm was referring to, but stalling for time.

"The sleepover?"

"Oh, right," said Mikey. "Erm…"

"It's OK," said Norm. "You can tell me. I don't mind."

"Really?" said Mikey.

"Really," said Norm.

"It was all right, I suppose."

"All right?" said Norm.

"OK, it was pretty good."

"Pretty good?"

Mikey sighed. "What do you want me to say, Norm?"

Norm thought for a moment. What he actually **wanted** Mikey to say was that he'd had a really **rubbish** time at Zak flipping Knight's. That all that talk of ninety-six-inch screens and inappropriate Xbox games and staying up all night had been precisely that. All talk. That's what Norm **wanted** Mikey to say.

"If you really **must** know, it was brilliant."

"Oh, thanks **very** much, Mikey!" said Norm.

"Well, you **did** ask, Norm! What did you expect me to do? Lie?"

Actually, thought Norm, that was **precisely** what he'd expected Mikey to do. But there was more chance of Norm giving up pizza than there was of Mikey ever telling a lie. Not even a little white lie in order to help make Norm feel a bit better. It just wasn't in Mikey's nature. It was **so** flipping annoying.

They cycled on in silence for a couple more minutes until they turned into the precinct.

"So what happened?" said Norm, skidding to a halt.

"What do you mean?" said Mikey, pulling up beside him.

"You **know** what I mean, Mikey," said Norm. "How come you ended up going to the allotments?"

Mikey suddenly looked very uncomfortable. "I can't remember."

"Mikey?" said Norm, raising one eyebrow.

"All right, all right!" said Mikey. "It's my fault!"

"Your fault?" said Norm.

"Zak mentioned something about you and that cauliflower you were carrying."

"And...?"

"And I might have mentioned something about where I thought you'd probably got it from."

"**Might** have mentioned?"

"OK, OK," said Mikey. "**Did** mention."

"I see," said Norm.

"How was I supposed to know we'd end up **going** there?" said Mikey, getting more and more upset. "I **tried** to stop him, Norm! Honest I did! But he suddenly saw the paint and the brush and the next thing..."

"Well, well, well," said a voice. "Fancy seeing **you** here."

Norm and Mikey looked round to see Alice Knight approaching them. And loitering a few steps behind her was none other than Zak flipping Knight.

"Er, yeah, fancy," said Norm hesitantly. "We were, er, just talking about you, actually."

"Me?" said Alice.

"Erm, Zak, actually."

"That's really funny," said Alice. "Because we were just talking about you, Norman. Weren't we, Zak?"

"What?" said Zak Knight, who up until that point had been staring intently at the ground.

"I said, we were just talking about Norman, weren't we?"

"Er, yeah."

"As a matter of fact, Zak's got something to say to you, Norman," said Alice. "Well, **both** of you actually."

Norm and Mikey glanced at each other. Events appeared to have taken an unexpected twist. It was **them** who were supposed to be having words with Zak Knight – not the other way round. But they'd been caught off guard.

"Zak?" said Alice expectantly.

"What?" said Zak Knight.

"I said, you've got something to say to Norman and Mikey, haven't you?"

"Er, yeah," mumbled Zak Knight. "Sorry."

Uh? thought Norm. Had he just heard what he **thought** he'd just heard? Had Zak Knight really just said he was **sorry**?

"Speak up, Zak," said Alice. "I don't think they could hear you."

"Sorry," said Zak, a bit louder.

"For what?"

"The graffiti."

"**And** for generally being a doughnut," added Alice.

Whoa, thought Norm. This was not only unexpected but pretty flipping amazing, too.

"How did you find out?" said Norm.

"About the graffiti, you mean?" said Alice.

Norm nodded.

"Well, the paint-splattered clothes were a bit of a giveaway," said Alice. "A couple of questions and it all came pouring out!"

Uh? thought Norm. **What** came pouring out? On second thoughts, thought Norm, perhaps he didn't want to know! And anyway – he was **still** no nearer finding out **why** Zak Knight had decided to customise Grandpa's shed in the first place. What **was** this grudge that Mikey reckoned Zak had all about? And what had it got to do with flipping sheep?

"Can I ask something?" said Norm.

"I've got a feeling I might know what it is," said Alice.

"Really?" said Norm.

Alice nodded. "Can you remember your first Christmas at primary school?"

Norm pulled a face. "Er, no. That wasn't what I was going to ask."

"I know it wasn't," said Alice. "But can you?"

What kind of ridiculous question was that? thought Norm. He could hardly remember what happened this time last flipping week, let alone his first Christmas at primary school! And what on earth had that got to do with anything, anyway?

"Well?" said Alice. "Can you?"

"Not really," said Norm.

"Me neither," said Mikey.

"Well, *Zak* can," said Alice. "Can't you, Zak?"

"Yeah," mumbled Zak, staring at the ground again.

"The nativity play?" said Alice.

Norm shrugged. "What about it?"

"You played the part of Joseph?"

"I did?" said Norm.

"Actually, yeah, you **did**, come to think of it, Norm," said Mikey. "I remember that now."

"What?" said Norm irritably. "How come **you** can remember, Mikey?"

"Just can," said Mikey.

"The thing is," said Alice, looking meaningfully at Zak, "apparently a certain somebody **else** wanted to play the part of Joseph."

Whoa, thought Norm. **Now** it looked like they were getting somewhere.

"Guess what part he got instead?" said Alice.

"Pardon?" said Norm.

"Guess what part Zak ended up playing?" said Alice. "Instead of Joseph?"

Norm thought for a moment. Everything suddenly made sense. **Perfect** sense! 'Revenge of the sheep'? 'BAAA!' painted on the side of Grandpa's shed?

"Well?" said Alice. "Any idea?"

"A sheep?" said Norm.

"Is the correct answer," said Alice.

Gordon flipping Bennet, thought Norm. **That** was why Zak had deliberately tried to wreck his friendship with Mikey? **That** was why he'd done his best to try and get Norm into trouble? **That** was why he'd been acting like a prize-winning doughnut? Because he couldn't forget something that had happened, like, a million years ago or something – and that Norm had no memory of whatso-flipping-ever? It was **such** a ridiculously **stupid** reason it was **almost** funny. But somehow, thought Norm, it wasn't actually funny at all. Somehow, thought Norm, instead of enjoying this moment and making the most of it like he **should** have been doing, there was a **teensy** part of him that couldn't help wondering what **he** would have felt like had things been the other way round – and **he'd** wanted to be Joseph but ended up being a sheep, and only had one parent. It was **so** flipping annoying, thought Norm. And **so** flipping unfair!

"Well, Norman?" said Alice. "Aren't you going to say something?"

"Sorry," said Norm.

"What?" said Zak Knight, looking up in surprise. "**You're** sorry?"

Norm nodded.

"What for?"

"For not being a sheep," said Norm. "And..."

"What?" said Zak Knight.

Norm briefly wondered whether to say what else he was sorry about. "Just, you know…"

"What?"

"Stuff," said Norm, glancing at Alice.

"Stuff?" said Zak Knight.

Norm nodded. "Stuff."

Norm and Zak Knight looked at each other. Not for long. But long enough to understand. Understand that whilst they might never be the best of buddies, whatever had been going on between them was over. For now, anyway.

"Let's go, Zak," said Alice.

"Where to?" said Zak Knight.

"What do you mean, where to?" said Alice, heading off. "Who do you **think's** going to paint that shed again? The Paint Fairy?"

Norm couldn't help chuckling.

"See you tomorrow, Cauliflower Boy," muttered Zak Knight, following after his sister.

"What?" said Norm. "Where?"

"At school."

Norm sighed. Just when he thought he'd actually had the *last* laugh. Zak flipping Knight had gone and had it instead. Flipping typical.

CHAPTER 24

Norm cycled home, unable to decide quite how he was supposed to be feeling. On the one hand it looked like he and Mikey were going to be OK after all. Well, it didn't *look* like they were going to be OK. They *were* going to be OK. Norm knew that for sure now. Normal service had been well and truly resumed.

On the other hand, thought Norm, turning into his street, it hadn't even *occurred* to him that Zak Knight would be going to the same flipping school as him and Mikey. What did he have to go and do *that* for? Why couldn't he go to another school? Wasn't it *enough* that he'd been the cause of so much hassle? Why did there *always* have to be a downside? wondered Norm. Why did there *always* have to be a flipping catch?

Norm turned into his drive, his mind still elsewhere. Had his mind **not** been elsewhere – and had he been concentrating a little harder on where he was going – Norm might actually have **noticed** John come shooting out of the front door, and then **not** had to swerve violently in order to avoid hitting him, before crashing into the fence.

"Ow," moaned Norm, lying on the ground. "Flipping dog."

"Hello, **Norman**," said Chelsea, instantly popping up on the other side of the fence.

For once though, it didn't irritate Norm that Chelsea had suddenly appeared out of the blue.

It wasn't like she'd barged, uninvited, into his house again while he was sitting on the toilet. He couldn't actually **stop** her being in her dad's garden. And besides, he was in too much pain to actually care.

"What are you doing?"

Norm sighed. "What does it flipping **look** like I'm doing? I've just crashed, haven't I?"

"What did you do **that** for?" said Chelsea.

"Gordon flipping Bennet!" said Norm. "I didn't **mean** to!"

"All right, **Norman**!" said Chelsea. "Keep your hair on!"

258

Norm managed to disentangle himself from underneath his bike and got slowly to his feet.

"Any damage?" asked Chelsea.

Norm nodded. "I've hurt my wrist."

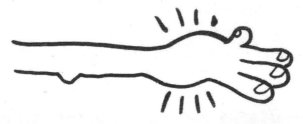

"I meant the **bike** – not you, **Norman!**"

"Very funny," muttered Norm, flexing his wrist. The **same** wrist he'd hurt twenty-four hours previously in **another** dog-related accident. And now it was **really** sore. And now Chelsea came to mention it, thought Norm, examining his bike, there **was** actually some damage. The front wheel was all buckled and bent. There'd be no more riding till **that** was fixed.

Unbelievable, thought Norm. Just unbe-flipping-lievable. It wasn't even lunchtime, and already today was making **yesterday** seem like a flipping picnic in the park by comparison. Surely it couldn't go on like this, could it? **Something** good had to happen sooner or later.

"Anyone seen John?" said Brian, appearing at the front door.

"Funny you should mention it," said Norm, glaring venomously at his middle brother.

"There he is," said Chelsea.

"Where?" said Brian.

"There," laughed Chelsea.

Norm turned round just in time to see John cock a leg and pee all over his bike.

 said Brian.

"Oops?" said Norm. "Is that all you've got to..."

Norm suddenly stopped, mid-sentence. He'd only just noticed what Brian was holding in his hand.

"Is that pizza?"

"Yeah," said Brian.

"Where did you get it from?"

"Found it," said Brian.

"Where?" said Norm.

"Under my bed," said Brian.

Norm grinned. Perhaps today wasn't going to turn out to be quite so bad after all.

Brian pulled a face. "What's so funny?"

Norm shrugged. "Nothing."

Want more Norm?
Read on for an extract from his first
hilarious adventure:

CHAPTER 1

Norm knew it was going to be one of those days when he woke up and found himself about to pee in his dad's wardrobe.

"Whoa! Stop Norman!" yelled Norm's dad, sitting bolt upright and switching on his bedside light.

"Uh? What?" mumbled Norm, his voice still thick with sleep.

"What do you think you're doing?"

"Having a pee?" said Norm, like this was the most stupid question in the entire history of stupid questions.

"Not in my wardrobe you're not!" said Norm's dad.

"That's from Ikea that is," added Norm's mum, like it was somehow OK to pee in a wardrobe that wasn't.

Norm was confused. The last thing he knew he'd been on the verge of becoming the youngest ever World Mountain Biking Champion, when he'd suddenly had to slam on his brakes to avoid hitting a tree. Now here he was having to slam on a completely different kind of brakes in order to avoid a completely different kind of accident. What was going on? And what were his parents doing sleeping in the bathroom anyway?

"Toilet's moved," said Norm, hopping from one foot to the other, something which at the age of three was considered socially acceptable, but which at the age of nearly thirteen, most definitely wasn't.

"What?" said Norm's dad.

"Toilet's moved," said Norm, a bit louder.

But Norm's dad had heard what Norm said. He just couldn't quite *believe* what Norm had said.

"No, Norman. It's not the *toilet* that's moved! It's *us* that's moved!"

"Forgot," said Norm.

Norm's dad looked at his eldest son. "Are you serious?"

"Yeah," said Norm, like this was the *second* most stupid question in the entire history of stupid questions.

"You *forgot* we moved house?"

"Yeah," said Norm.

"How can you *forget* we moved house?" said Norm's dad, increasingly incredulous.

"Just did," shrugged Norm, increasingly close to wetting himself.

"But we moved over three months ago, Norman!" said Norm's dad.

"Three months, two weeks and five days ago, to be precise," said Norm's mum, like she hadn't even had to think about it.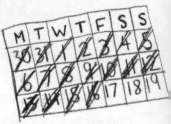

Norm's dad sighed wearily and looked at his watch. It was two o'clock in the morning.

"Look, Norman. You just can't go round peeing in other peoples' wardrobes and that's all there is to it!"

"I didn't," said Norm.

"No, but you were *about* to!"

Norm's dad was right. Norm *had* been about to pee in the wardrobe, but he'd managed to stop himself just in time.

Typical, thought Norm. Being blamed for something he hadn't actually done.

Norm considered arguing the point, but by now his bladder felt like it was the size of a space hopper. If he didn't pee soon he was going to explode. Then he'd *really* be in trouble!

"Go on. Clear off," said Norm's dad.

Norm didn't need telling twice and began waddling towards the door like a pregnant penguin.

"Oh, and Norman?"

"Yeah?" said Norm without bothering to stop.

"The toilet's at the end of the corridor. You can't miss it."

Norm didn't reply. He knew that if he didn't get to the toilet in the next ten seconds there was a very good chance that he *would* miss it!

CHAPTER 2

Norm tried every trick he knew to get back to sleep. The trouble was, Norm only knew one trick – counting sheep jumping over a gate – and it just wasn't working. For a start he'd made the gate much too high. There was no way a sheep was going to be able to clear it. Not without some kind of springboard or mini trampoline, anyway. In the end there was a big pile-up of sheep, all milling about like...well, sheep, basically. It was so annoying. And the more Norm thought about it the less sleepy he got. And the less sleepy Norm got the less chance there was of carrying on the dream where he'd left off. Was he destined to become World Mountain Biking Champion or not?

Norm was desperate to find out.

Norm tried to guess what time it was. The last time he'd looked it had been 2.30. That seemed like ages ago. But it was hard to tell. It was still pitch black outside. A couple of cars had driven up and down the street and some random guy had wandered past, singing tunelessly at the top of his voice. Norm opened one eye to check. The red digits of the digital clock glowed, suspended in the dark.

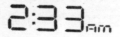

Norm couldn't believe it. Three minutes? Was that *really* all it had been since he'd last looked? Three measly minutes? A hundred and eighty stupid seconds? A twentieth of a flipping hour? No way, thought Norm. That can't be right. The clock must be faulty. The battery must have run out. The world must have stopped turning. There *had* to be a rational explanation. It couldn't possibly have been only *three* minutes! But it was. He was never *ever* going to get back to sleep at this rate!

It didn't help that Norm could hear his dad, snoring away like a constipated rhinoceros. Not that Norm had ever actually heard a constipated rhinoceros – but he imagined that's what one would have sounded like. He'd never noticed how loud it was before. Before they'd moved house, that is. Their old house had been solid and sound proof. There could literally have *been* a constipated rhinoceros in their old house and Norm wouldn't have heard it. But in this house, with its tiny rooms and paper-thin walls, you could virtually hear fingernails growing.

Norm tried putting his pillow over his head but it didn't make the slightest bit of difference. It was an incredible racket. It wouldn't have been so bad,

but his mum and dad's room wasn't even next to Norm's! How come his mum could sleep through it and yet Norm couldn't? How come his stupid little brothers could sleep through it and yet Norm couldn't? It was just so unfair, thought Norm. But then so was everything these days.

Like being blamed for peeing in his dad's wardrobe for instance. Or rather, *not* peeing in his dad's wardrobe. How unfair was that? It wasn't Norm's fault they'd moved was it? It would never have happened in their old house. In their old house he'd never once woken up to find himself about to pee in anything *other* than a toilet. In their old house Norm would have been back to sleep ages ago!

The more Norm thought about it, the more wound up he got. Why on earth did they have to go and move in the first place? Who in their right minds would leave a nice big house for a glorified rabbit hutch? Well, not exactly big.

It wasn't like it was massive or anything. But compared to this place their old house was like Buckingham flipping Palace! It just didn't make sense to Norm.

And yes, Norm *knew* there were homeless people out there who'd give anything to have a roof over their heads and that he shouldn't be so ungrateful and all that stuff. His mum and dad didn't need to tell him *that*. Just like they didn't need to keep banging on about starving children in Africa every time he left a bit of broccoli, but they still did. If they were *that* bothered why didn't they just bung it in a jiffy bag and send it to them?

And how was Norm ever supposed to become World Mountain Biking Champion eating flipping broccoli anyway?

By now, Norm was oozing anger. The air around him practically crackled, as if he was some kind of human electricity generator. Never mind flipping wind-farms or solar flipping panels. If harnessed correctly, Norm could have single-handedly powered a small town for a whole year!

It was probably just as well then that Norm *didn't* hear Brian, his middle brother, pad along the landing and open his parents' bedroom door. It was probably just as well that he *wasn't* there to see Brian lift the lid of the laundry basket and pee in it. And it was *definitely* just as well that Norm *didn't* see Brian pad away again without so much as a peep from his parents, one of whom was still snoring like a constipated rhinoceros and the other of whom was busy dreaming of her next trip to IKEA.

A car drove down the street, the beam of its headlights flickering through a crack in the curtains and briefly illuminating Norm's face. But amazingly, Norm never even noticed. Like a hurricane that had finally blown itself out, Norm had fallen fast and furiously asleep.

The *good* news as far as Norm was concerned was that he picked up the dream exactly where he'd left off. The *bad* news was that his best friend Mikey became the youngest ever World Mountain Biking Champion. Norm came second. It was *so* unfair.

CHAPTER 3

Norm gradually became aware of the sound of muffled voices. What on earth could his mum and dad be talking about at this time? It was the middle of the flipping night! Surely whatever it was could wait till morning couldn't it?

Norm opened an eye and looked at the clock.

10:14 am

Norm closed his eye again and snuggled back into the duvet. By now he was beginning to make out occasional random words and phrases like *stainless steel, dishwasher friendly* and *twelve easy monthly payments.*

His parents really should get out more, decided Norm.

The fog of Norm's mind slowly began to clear. Something didn't quite compute. Something wasn't quite right. But what?

Norm sat up and looked out the window. It was light outside.

Funny, thought Norm. How come it was light in the middle of the night? Was there like an eclipse or something and nobody had bothered to tell him? He wouldn't be surprised. Nobody bothered to tell Norm anything. It could literally be the end of the world and Norm would be the last to find out.

Norm opened an eye again and looked at the clock.

10:15 am

The penny still didn't drop immediately, but when it finally did, it dropped with an almighty clunk. There wasn't an eclipse. It wasn't the middle of the night any more. It was actually the middle of the morning. It looked like Norm *had* got back to sleep after all!

"Aaaaaaaaaaggggh!!" screamed Norm, leaping out of bed.

There was a sudden rush of footsteps up the stairs. By the time Norm's mum appeared at the door, Norm was in his pants and hopping round the room trying to put his socks on.

"Are you OK, love?" said Norm's mum in a tone that suggested that at the very least she'd been expecting to find Norm lying in a heap on the floor, possibly even gushing blood.

"No, I am *not* OK, actually!" said Norm. "Why didn't you wake me, Mum?"

"Because it's Saturday," said Norm's mum, matter-of-factly.

But Norm wasn't listening.

"How am I supposed to get to school on time if nobody wakes me? It wasn't *my* fault I overslept! It wouldn't have happened if we lived in a *proper* house! How am I supposed to sleep with that flipping racket going on? Honestly, it's a miracle the neighbours haven't phoned to complain! Mind you, they don't actually *need* to phone do they? They can just shout!"

SHUT UP!

neighbour

Norm stopped, but only because he needed to breathe. His mum just smiled, which somehow made Norm even angrier.

"I'm serious, Mum! The walls are so flipping thin you can hear a spider fart three rooms away!"

Norm's mum laughed.

"It's not funny!" said Norm.

"I know it's not, love."

"So why are you laughing?"

"Because it's Saturday, Norman."

 said Norm.

"It's Saturday," said Norm's mum. *"That's* why we didn't wake you."

"You might've said."

"I did."

Norm looked at his mum for a moment.

"Is this a wind-up Mum? It really *is* Saturday?"

Norm's mum smiled again.

"You don't honestly think we'd let you sleep in on a school day do you, Norman?"

It was a fair point, thought Norm. His parents were weird, but not *that* weird. It really *was* Saturday.

Norm felt both relieved and happy. Not only was he *not* late for school, he didn't actually have to *go* to school! And as if that wasn't brilliant enough, Norm suddenly remembered that Mikey was coming round to bike! Things just didn't get any better than that!

"You can go back to bed if you like, love," said Norm's mum.

"Where's everybody else?" said Norm.

"At the supermarket," said Norm's mum.

Norm looked puzzled. "So – who were you talking to just now?"

"Nobody."

"Yeah you were," said Norm. "I heard voices."

"Shopping channels," said Norm's mum.

"Shopping channels?" said Norm.

"Yeah."

That explained the random words then, thought Norm. He might have known. His mum was buying more and more stuff off the telly these days.

"Well?" said Norm's mum, expectantly.

"Well what?" said Norm, even though he knew perfectly well what that particular *well* meant.

"Aren't you going to ask me if I bought anything?"

Norm knew his mum would tell him whether he asked or not. He might as well get it over with.

"Did you buy anything, Mum?"

"Set of saucepans."

Norm looked at his mum. "But..."

"But what love?"

"We've already *got* saucepans."

"Yes, I know. But it was a bargain!"

"Yes, but we don't actually *need* any more saucepans, Mum."

Norm's mum looked at Norm with an almost pitying expression. "No, you don't *understand* Norman. It was a *bargain!*"

Norm's mum was right. Norm *didn't* understand. Why buy something just because it was a bargain? What was the point if you didn't *need* it? Like that bulk load of dog food currently taking up most of the shed. Norm could hardly get his bike in and out. He wouldn't have minded, but they didn't actually *have* a dog.

"By the way," said Norm's mum, "did you know you've got your pants on the wrong way round?"

Norm sighed. Of *course* he didn't know he'd got his flipping pants on the wrong way round! Why would anyone *deliberately* do that? All the same Norm was actually quite glad that he *had* put his pants on the wrong way round. They were the ones with *May Contain Nuts* written on the front.

If you like The World of Norm, you'll love

978 1 40831 511 8 £5.99

978 1 40831 512 5 £5.99

"Hilarious stuff from one of my comic heroes!"
Harry Hill

Just when Norm thought life couldn't get any more unfair...

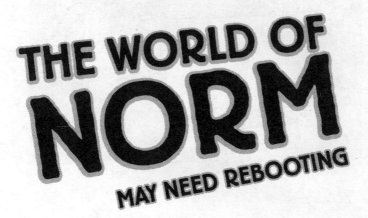

THE WORLD OF NORM
MAY NEED REBOOTING

COMING SOON!

ORCHARD BOOKS
www.orchardbooks.co.uk